D0975397

BOOKS BY DEAN HUGHES

Nutty for President

Honestly, Myron

Switching Tracks

*Millie Willenheimer
and the Chestnut Corporation*

*Nutty and the Case of
the Mastermind Thief*

*Nutty and the Case of
the Ski-Slope Spy*

Nutty
and the Case
of the
Ski-Slope Spy

Nutty and the Case of the Ski-Slope Spy

Featuring William Bilks

BOY GENIUS

by Dean Hughes

HEARST FREE LIBRARY
ANACONDA, MONTANA

Atheneum   1985   New York

For
Bryant & Linda Nelson,
Matt, Clark, Leigh, Shelly,
Jenny & Bill

Library of Congress Cataloging in Publication Data

Hughes, Dean.
Nutty and the case of the ski-slope spy.

SUMMARY: After finding mysterious plans in their hotel
bathroom, Nutty and his friends must avoid imposters who
want the papers and danger on the ski
slopes.
1. Children's stories, American. [1. Skis and
skiing—Fiction. 2. Spies—Fiction. 3. Mystery and
detective stories] I. Title.
PZ7.H87312Nt 1985 [Fic] 85-7962
ISBN 0-689-31126-5

Copyright © 1985 by Dean Hughes
All rights reserved
Published simultaneously in Canada by
Collier Macmillan Canada, Inc.
Type Set by Heritage Printers, Inc., Charlotte, North Carolina
Printed and bound by Fairfield Graphics, Fairfield, Pennsylvania
Designed by Mary Ahern
First Edition

Contents

Nutty
and the Case
of the
Ski-Slope Spy

Chapter 1

The
Wedge Position

Orlando was looking out the airplane window, occasionally commenting about all the snow in the mountains. "Skiing is going to be my sport," he said. "I'm going to be great."

Nutty Nutsell, who was sitting on the aisle, whispered to his friend Bilbo, "It's not as easy as he thinks."

"I heard that," Orlando said, and he twisted around to look at Nutty. "Maybe it wasn't easy for you to learn. But you don't happen to have my athletic ability. I pick up things very quick, you know."

"Yes—bad grammar, for instance," William Bilks mumbled. He was sitting across the aisle from Nutty, and he had his nose in a book.

"Actually, I'm sort of nervous about skiing,"

Bilbo said. "If I can't catch on to it, this isn't going to be a very fun trip."

William heard this and leaned into the aisle as far as he could. "Bilbo, you may want to borrow this book." He held it up, and Nutty saw the title: *The Basics of Skiing for the Beginner.* "I've been reading it this morning, and it's really quite helpful. Once a person masters the wedge position—the 'snowplow'—he can get by pretty well. I'm not an athlete by any means, but I'm not too concerned."

Nutty was not so sure that William wasn't an athlete. He was little and plump, but he could do anything he put his mind to. And what a mind! The kid was a genius—that's all there was to it. Orlando, however, leaned around Bilbo and said, "William, you've got to be kidding. You can't learn how to ski from a book."

"Of course not. But I'm learning the theory. That will help when we start our lessons. We get our first lesson today, don't we Nutty?"

"Yeah. At two o'clock. All we do is check in at the lodge and have lunch—and then we head for Big Mama."

"Big Mama?"

Nutty laughed. "That's where you take your lesson—at the base of Big Mama. It's the name of a ski run."

4

"That's good to know," Orlando said. "I thought maybe that was the name of our ski instructor."

Nutty was just smiling now. He leaned back and relaxed. He felt great. He had finally done something right. Lots of kids had said he wasn't a very good Student Council president, but this ski trip—from Missouri all the way out to Utah—was going to improve his reputation. Nutty had negotiated a good deal. The flight, lodging, meals, ski rental, lessons—everything—came as part of one package price. True, it was plenty of money, but some had gotten the trip as a Christmas present and others had raised a lot of the money on their own.

However the kids had managed it, twenty-two had come up with the money, and they, along with four chaperons, were on their way to five days of skiing. It was the day after Christmas, and all reports were that the snow was deep this year.

So everything was perfect. Lessons were scheduled, lodge rooms reserved, bus transportation arranged. Added to that, Nutty had been going west on an annual ski trip with his parents for years, so he was likely to be the best skier in the group. At this point, it really appeared that nothing could go wrong.

"Oh man, we're free at last," Orlando said. "Our own condo room for five days. No parents around. No school work. We can just kick back and—"

Orlando looked up. A throat was being cleared, just above his head. Mrs. Ash was looking over the top of the seat. "Maybe your parents aren't here, but I am. And I told your mom I'd keep a sharp eye on you. So don't start singing 'Free at Last' quite yet."

Mrs. Ash was a big woman, tall and strong, with a boisterous laugh. She looked over at Nutty and gave him a wink. Orlando just moaned and then went back to looking out the window.

"Don't worry, Mrs. Ash," William said from across the aisle. "I'll keep a careful watch on Orlando. I know how his mind works—slowly, if at all."

Orlando spun around and gave William a dirty look.

"Yes, and who'll keep a watch on you, William?" Mrs. Ash said. "Dr. Dunlop didn't even like the idea of your going along."

"That's only because I don't go to your school any more."

"I'd say that's one of the reasons." No one needed to comment any further. They all knew that William had experienced some run-ins with the principal. Nutty had practically had to beg Dr. Dunlop to let William go along. And finally it had been Mrs. Ash herself who had said she would keep a special watch on the little genius.

"I believe," William said, "that finding the minimum number was something of a problem and that Dr. Dunlop finally decided that my dollars were as good as any others."

"William," Mrs. Ash said, "just let me say this. Every time you solve a problem for us, you seem to create a dozen. Would you just ski on this trip and leave the problems to the chaperones?"

"But of course. I wouldn't want it any other way."

Nutty had to smile. He knew exactly what Mrs. Ash was talking about. But he wasn't worried this time. Things had gone very smoothly so far.

In fact, the whole day went just as well as Nutty had hoped it would. The airplane landed on time in Salt Lake City; the bus was at the airport to pick them up and transport them to the ski resort; the rooms at the lodge were ready; and the kids made it to their lesson on time. Mrs. Ash had nothing but praise for Nutty's organizational skills. Nutty told her, quite humbly, that the travel agent had taken care of most everything, but he still enjoyed hearing the compliments.

Nutty, along with the other kids who had skied before, went straight to the Big Mama chairlift. The others took their beginner lesson on the relatively flat area at the base of the mountain. And they did very well. Or at least most of them did. There was one who seemed to have more than his share of trouble.

When all the kids were on the back of the shuttle truck, heading back to the lodge, Orlando was looking pretty down in the mouth. "I think there was something wrong with those skis they rented me," he said. Some of the guys started to laugh. "No, really. I think I had defective equipment."

A couple of the girls started teasing Orlando, and one of the sixth-grade boys asked whether he was still planning to enter the Olympics.

"Actually, I think there was something wrong," Nutty said. "I think the guy at the rental place attached them wrong."

"Do you really think so?" Orlando said. He sounded hopeful.

"Yeah, I honestly do. I think he attached them to your feet—that was his first mistake."

The kids all cracked up, but Orlando didn't find Nutty's comment very funny. He was at the front of the truck, leaning against the cab, and he looked exhausted. "Yeah, you laugh now, but wait until tomorrow. I'm going to get the kind of skis William had. His worked the way they're supposed to from the minute he put them on. If I get the same kind, I'll be better than anyone. I'm a better athlete than William."

This brought on a barrage of comments again,

mostly put-downs from the older kids. They didn't like a fifth grader being quite so cocky. But then William spoke, and he sounded serious. "Orlando, I have the impression that you've picked up some bad habits from watching television."

"You mean from watching ski racers?"

"Well, no. I was thinking of one of those nature shows—Wild Kingdom and that sort of thing."

"William, what are you talking about?"

"Well, as I watched you today, I noticed something in your approach, a flaw in your technique. And I was reminded of something I once saw on one of those shows." He paused and seemed to consider, then he nodded. "Yes, I'm sure of it. You looked exactly the same."

"The same as what?"

"Well . . . it was a goose, an enormous one, and it was trying to walk on ice."

The truck had just pulled up in front of the lodge, but for a moment no one started to climb down. They were all laughing too hard. Even Mrs. Ash and her husband were laughing, and so were the other two chaperones, Mr. and Mrs. Crawford. The Crawfords were parents of one of the sixth-grade girls, and they were excellent skiers. They had tried to help Orlando, so they knew exactly what William was talking about.

Orlando was saying, "Funny. Very funny, William. You just wait until tomorrow." He stayed where he was until everyone else got off the truck, and then he trudged along behind them.

Nutty did feel a little sorry for him, even if he was getting what he deserved after all his bragging. But Orlando would catch on sooner or later. Nutty wasn't too worried about that. Right now nothing could ruin his good mood. The skiing had been great, and there would be lots more ahead. And next there would be a nice meal and a relaxing evening with his buddies.

That's what he was thinking as he walked down the hall toward his room. But William, who was walking ahead, suddenly came to a stop. And then as Nutty and the other boys came up behind him, they saw why. The door to their room was open, and three men were inside.

A tall man wearing a three-piece suit turned and looked at the boys. "Oh, hello there. Are you the boys registered in this room?" He looked serious, and so did the other two men.

"Yes," William said.

"I'm the manager. I'm sorry that we had to enter your room this way."

"What's going on?" Nutty said.

"Well . . . these men are police officers. They're having a look around. And they'd like to talk to you."

Nutty felt a certain weakness in his knees, not entirely from the afternoon of skiing. His perfect day seemed to be heading for a lousy ending.

Chapter 2

A Bug
in the Room

Nutty glanced over at Orlando, who had taken a sudden breath and now was staring at the two policemen. But William stepped forward. "What can we do for you?" he said.

"Are you Frederick Nutsell?"

"No, sir. I'm William Bilks. This is Mr. Nutsell here."

Nutty's heart started to pound. What did these guys want? "Sir, I'm sure I haven't done anything—"

"No, no. It's not that. Yours was the only name I knew. You signed the registration card. The officers were simply wondering whether you boys noticed anything out of the ordinary when you checked in the room?"

"Out of the ordinary?" William said. "What sort of thing?"

One of the policemen, a stout man wearing a top coat and holding a hat in his hand, said, "Nothing specific. Just anything that seemed strange. Or was there, by chance, anything left in the room? Does everything here belong to you boys?"

Nutty looked around. But William said, "Yes. I'm sure it does. I noticed nothing here when we came in." He looked around at Bilbo and Orlando. "You fellows didn't see anything, did you?"

"Just towels and soap and—"

"No, no," the manager said. "We were thinking more in terms of personal belongings from a previous guest."

All the boys shook their heads, and Nutty said, "The room was all cleaned up and everything. Did you ask the maid whether she saw anything?"

"Well, yes. Of course. But the bed had not been slept in, so she really didn't have much to do. We just thought she might have missed something somehow."

"Did someone lose something? What should we be watching for?"

"Uh . . . well, nothing in particular. But we do want to look around a little more. You boys can stay here. We won't be long."

The police officers continued to look, inspecting things with obvious care. They pulled drawers all the way out, checked the undersides, and practically took the beds apart.

This seemed rather strange to Nutty, but he was relieved to know that he was in no trouble. He took a seat and just watched the policemen search. In a few minutes Mrs. Ash came by. "Oh, hello," she said, seeming surprised to see the men in the room.

"Hello," the manager said. "Are you the leader of this group?"

"I'm one of them."

"I see. These men are police officers. They're just having a look around the room." He must have seen the startled look on her face. "Don't worry— the boys haven't done anything wrong. We're just . . . doing some checking. A man who stayed in the room until last night is missing."

"Missing?"

"Yes, ma'am. He left the lodge last night, although he had reservations until this morning. And he wasn't on his scheduled flight home today. We're just trying to see whether there's any hint here as to what happened to him."

"Well, there's probably some simple explanation," Mrs. Ash said. She glanced around at the boys, obviously trying to look confident.

"Yes, we hope so. But he did call his wife last

night and say some . . . rather curious things. That's why the officers were called in." Mrs. Ash nodded, but she seemed uneasy. "In any case, we'll be finished soon and the boys will have their room." He turned around and looked toward Bilbo. "So how was the skiing today?"

Bilbo said something about just learning, and the manager gave a little pitch about Utah having the best snow in the world; but Nutty wasn't paying much attention. He was watching one of the policemen, who had just discovered something behind a picture frame. Nutty didn't get much of a look at it, but he saw that it was a small metal object. The officer pulled it loose and then hid it in his hand as he walked over to the other policeman. He showed the other man what he had found, but he was careful not to let anyone else see it.

The two policemen whispered for a minute, and then one turned to the manager and said, "Is there another room where the boys could stay tonight?"

"Oh, no, I'm sorry. This whole week is booked solid. We don't have a single extra room."

The officers both nodded, and the stout one said, "Well, that's fine. Maybe they could go down and get something to eat now, if they would like; we'll be finished here before long." Nutty thought the man seemed a little nervous now.

All the same, the boys went down, still wearing

their ski clothes, and had their dinner. Some of the other kids from their group were there too, but William suggested to the boys that they take a rather distant table. Once they were seated, he leaned forward and whispered, "Nutty, you saw what I did, didn't you?"

"You mean the thing behind the picture?"

"Yes."

"What was it?"

"It was a listening device. I'm certain of it."

"You mean the room was bugged?" Bilbo said.

"It would appear so."

"Why?"

There was a long pause, and then Orlando said, "Hey, that cop wanted to get us out of there. How come?"

"Probably so he could inspect the room more carefully—without our seeing anything," William said. "I really don't think we're in any danger. I don't see why we should be."

Even so, the boys were a little uneasy. When a couple of the sixth-grade girls came over to the table and asked Orlando to do his "goose imitation," Orlando told them to lay off, but he lacked his usual intensity.

After the boys went back to their room—and found the policemen gone—they all sat down and tried to act as if nothing had happened. But each was taking a survey of things. Finally Orlando whispered, "You don't think anyone could be listening to us now, do you?"

"I assume not," William said. "I suppose more than one bug is possible. The police could have missed one somewhere. But it's not very likely."

"Oh, come on," Nutty said, "that's stupid. There was one. It's gone. Some guy disappeared. That's too bad, but it doesn't affect us. Let's just have a good time and forget the whole thing. I'm going to take a shower."

He got up and went into the bathroom. Though he was not quite so relaxed as he pretended, he did believe what he had said. He got into the shower and really enjoyed the warm water.

After a couple of minutes, however, he found a new annoyance. The drain was not working very well, and the stall was filling with water. He turned off the shower and gradually the water went down, but very slowly.

When the water was finally gone, he looked down at the drain. There seemed to be something in the pipe, under the drain cover. So he knelt down to look more closely and noticed that the screws in the cover were both loose.

The screws came out easily, and what he saw in the drain seemed to be a plastic bag. He worked his fingers down the pipe and slowly pulled the thing out.

17

It was the type of bag used to line a small wastepaper basket; and there was something in it: a roll of paper. Nutty's first thought was that it was a newspaper. He couldn't believe it. Was this someone's idea of a joke? But he didn't take a careful look, just tossed the whole thing out on the bathroom floor and then finished his shower.

Later, as he dressed, however, he began to wonder. The policemen had been looking for something out of the ordinary. Newspapers don't normally find their way into drain pipes. And when he retrieved the roll of paper to have a look at it again, he could see that it was not a newspaper at all. But the paper had gotten damp and wouldn't come apart very easily. So he couldn't tell what it really was.

He walked out then to show the other guys what he had found, and William was immediately curious. He took the paper back into the bathroom and used Nutty's hair dryer on it. Nutty watched for a time, but the process was slow. He lost patience and went back out to see what Bilbo and Orlando were doing. Bilbo was sprawled across the bed, his eyes closed. Orlando was watching TV.

"Weren't there any wildlife shows on?" Nutty asked.

"Shut up," Orlando said, refusing to look at Nutty. "Is the shower free now?"

"Yeah, but William's in there drying out that roll of paper."

"What for?"

"To see what it is."

"You gotta be kidding. Tell him to dry it out here. I wanta take a shower. I think someone sneaked up on me while I wasn't looking and did a tap dance on my body. I'm in pain, man. I mean, real pain."

Bilbo said, "It was the mountain."

"What was the mountain?"

"It was the mountain that jumped on you. I saw the whole thing. It got me a couple of times, too."

But Orlando was now looking the other way. William was standing near the bathroom door, motioning for the guys to come over to him.

"What do you want?" Orlando said.

William put his finger to his lips, signaling for silence, and again he motioned for them to come over to him.

Nutty said, "Hey, Bilbo, come here a sec."

Bilbo sat up and said, "What for?" And then he saw William, still motioning. The boys finally all moved toward William, who directed them to the little balcony outside their room.

It was cold out there, but William slid the door shut. "Listen," he whispered, "the room may not be bugged now, but we can't take any chances."

"Chances?" Orlando said. "What chances? Come on, William, don't start your—"

"Listen to me. Those papers—the ones that were down the drain—they're important documents."

"Are you sure?" Bilbo said.

"Yes. They're marked 'classified.' They're designs for some sort of computer hardware."

"We better call those policemen and tell them," Nutty said.

"No. We can't do that. There was a note scribbled across the inside page."

"A note?"

"Yes. I'll read it to you, but softly. Lean close to me." The boys' steaming breaths mingled as they huddled in a tight circle, and William read:

FINDER:
Don't destroy these papers. Don't give them to anyone. *My life depends on them. You have my life in your hands. I will return for them as soon as I can. I'll use the code name Russian Roulette. Be extremely careful for your own safety. I will try to reach you no later than*

"Than what?"

"The note stops. He must have stuck the papers down the pipe in a hurry and gotten out."

"Or maybe someone got to him."

"Yeah. Maybe."

"What do we do?"

"I'm not sure. I need to think. Go back in and shower and talk and watch television. Be normal. We've already been silent too long."

"Wait a minute," Orlando said. "Do you think people will be looking for these things? Will they come back here?"

"I don't know. It's a possibility. But for right now we have to assume that the room could still be bugged, or that we could be in a dangerous spot. Therefore, it's important that we do nothing that could be seen as out of the ordinary."

"What if someone's watching from the outside?" Bilbo said. "They'd be wondering what we're doing right now—out here on this balcony."

"Yes, that very thought just crossed my mind. Let's get back inside."

Nutty took a quick look around. The parking lot, three floors below, was covered with snow—deep snow. Most of the cars looked only like dunes of sand on a glowing white beach. Directly below was a great drift of powdery snow that reached halfway to their balcony. But all was quiet; no one was in sight. And yet Nutty felt a chill go through him. Maybe the cold was finally getting to him. Maybe he was just imagining things. But once inside, he found that acting "normal" was no easy task. He kept thinking of the words in the note: ". . . my life is in your hands . . . Be extremely careful for your own safety."

It was almost too much to believe. This was supposed to be his perfect five days—nothing but good snow and good times. He really didn't need anyone's life in his hands—and he certainly didn't want to have to worry about his own.

Chapter 3

Scared in
the Dark

It was not a fun evening. The plan had been for the
boys to kick back, eat a little junk food, watch a little
TV, or play some cards—but above all, to enjoy
being on their own. Now, however, Nutty found himself wishing his parents were with him, that he didn't
have to face this situation with guys his own age.

Orlando was even more upset. He kept telling
the guys not to sweat it, to have a good time. But he
was more tense than anyone. He couldn't sit still. He
must have walked to the glass doors and looked out
fifty times during the evening, and he couldn't seem
to get interested in anything on TV.

Having William around, however, was almost
like having an adult. He spent much of his time lost
in thought. Nutty knew that he was running every-

thing through his mind, considering every piece of data—just like a computer. He would have a plan developed before long. And that was sort of comforting. The only thing was, William liked stuff like this a little too much. Nutty didn't know what was more bothersome—watching Orlando pace around, or seeing William just sit there in his dull gray sweater, like a little old grandpa, with a hint of a smile on his face.

Eventually William gave the guys some clue as to what had been going through his head. He walked over and stood between the two beds and motioned for the boys to come closer. Bilbo was stretched out on one bed, and Nutty was sitting on the other. Orlando was momentarily perched in a chair. But all three came and sat on the edge of the beds, and William stood in between.

"Okay, now listen," William whispered.

"I can't hear you."

William rolled his eyes. "Orlando, lean in closer. I don't dare talk out loud."

Orlando nodded, and then he glanced around the room, as though he were trying to spot another listening device.

"I've tried to think of everything," William said. "I would like to discuss the whole matter with you, but now is not the time. Nutty, say something out loud."

"What?"

"Just say something—anything you might say under ordinary conditions. We want things to seem normal in here."

Nutty just stared at William for a moment. He couldn't think of one thing to say. And then he came out with, "Boy, the slopes should be great tomorrow."

Orlando shook his head, and Bilbo started to smile. William said, "Yes, I think they will be," but then he added in a whisper, "Nutty, don't ever try out for a school play, all right? Acting is not your greatest talent."

Nutty just shrugged. What did those guys expect? He wasn't exactly in a relaxed state.

"Never mind. Just listen. I don't think it would be wise to keep the documents in the room. Someone could force his way in here, and we would have no way to stop him. But I think it might even be more dangerous to leave the room—especially if we had the papers with us."

"So what are we supposed to do?" Orlando said.

"I have a plan. I'm going to use a wire hanger from the closet. I'll stick it through and around the papers to keep them in a tight cylinder. Then I'll place them on the balcony for a while until they freeze. They're still fairly wet, so that will be easy enough. After we turn off the lights to go to bed, I'll slip out onto the balcony and drop the documents into the snow drift below. That should put them in a deep freeze. We'll know where they are, so we can get them some time if we have to. But they'll be out of our hands."

"What if they stick in the snow but don't go all the way in?" Bilbo said. "They would be sticking right up there where someone could see them."

"I know. That's my greatest concern. But I took a good look at the snow. The top foot or foot and a half is just powdery stuff—new snow. It hasn't crusted over. The frozen papers should be heavy enough to drop right in. I think it's a chance we can afford to take."

"What if someone's keeping an eye on us from outside?" Nutty said. "If they saw you drop them, that would be that."

"I know. That's another serious concern. But I've watched the moon. It's on its way down. It'll be good and dark in two or three hours. I'll lie on my stomach and slide the door back. Then I'll inch out and just let the papers drop over the edge. With any luck, a little wind or a little new snow will hide the hole in the snow. That's got to be better than having them in here."

The boys were silent for a time, all staring at William. There had been something really frightening about the tone of those last words. Finally

Orlando said, "What's so bad about having the documents in here?"

"Think about it. Russian Roulette said that his life depends on them. Maybe ours do, too. Once we hand them over to someone, we are simply witnesses —and a danger to those who want the papers. But until then, we're worth more alive."

"Come on, William," Nutty said, "you read too many spy stories. No one's going to kill us. We're just . . . well, you know. No one wants to kill kids."

"I hope you're right. Chances are, you are right. But I don't like to take chances. Not with my life."

Silence again. Bilbo was nodding, seeming to agree. Orlando was staring, obviously scared stiff. Nutty could hear his own heart pounding in his ears.

And then someone knocked on the door. Nutty saw William go rigid for a second and then seem to find his senses. He spun around and headed for the bathroom. "Don't open the door," he hissed. "I'll drop the documents now if I have to."

Nutty had never seen William rattled like this. It was the last thing he needed right now. William was their best hope.

"Stall," William whispered, as he came back from the bathroom. "Ask who it is."

"Who is it?" Nutty asked, his voice sounding strained.

A voice boomed through the door. "It's the room inspector. I'm here to check you boys out." And then there was a big laugh.

It was Mrs. Ash.

Nutty took a deep breath, felt his chest relax a little, but he was still shaking. William spoke quickly. "Make sure she's alone before you let her in."

Orlando got to the door first. He seemed more than eager to see an adult. But he only pulled the door open a crack, and then he slammed it shut again. "What's the matter?" Bilbo said.

"She's not alone." Orlando was looking at William. "Should I open it?"

Nutty felt his chest grab again.

"Who's with her?" William said. By now the knocking had begun again.

"Mr. Ash."

Suddenly William grinned. "That's okay," he said. "I meant . . . well, you know."

But Nutty knew that Orlando wasn't thinking straight at the moment. His eyes were like stones. All the same, he turned and opened the door.

"What's going on?" Mrs. Ash said, and she peeked in around the door.

Orlando just stared at her, but William, from across the room, said, "I wasn't quite fully dressed." (This was a little strange, since he was standing

28

there in his sweater, and it was buttoned all the way up.)

"Oh, excuse me." Mrs. Ash laughed. Mr. Ash stepped in behind his wife. He was a fairly tall man, as tall as his wife, but not quite so powerful looking. He nodded to the boys. "So how is everything going?" Mrs. Ash asked.

"Fine. Just fine," William said, and he sounded natural enough. But Nutty felt the tenseness in the room.

"Well, you guys look a little guilty to me. You aren't throwing water balloons or anything like that, are you?"

"We forgot to bring any," Nutty said. He tried to laugh. At the moment, however, he was a little concerned about his acting ability.

"Mrs. Ash," Orlando said, "where—exactly— is your room?" His voice was as tight as a violin string.

"We're just down the hall," she said.

"Room 208," her husband added.

Mrs. Ash was looking carefully at Orlando. "Do you need anything, or—"

"No." Orlando glanced at William. Nutty knew what he wanted to do. He wanted to spill the whole story.

"To tell the truth," William said, "I think Orlando has gotten a little homesick. He's never been this far away before."

But Orlando didn't like that. "I am not," he said. "I'm fine."

The Ashes both laughed. "Are you still planning to be a ski racer, Orlando?" Mr. Ash asked.

This only angered Orlando all the more, but at least he walked away and sat down. And the other boys started to relax. After that Mrs. Ash simply gave what seemed to be a standard line of little warnings and then wished the boys good night and left.

When the door shut, Orlando spun around to William. "What did you say that for?"

"It was merely an attempt to give some logical explanation for your distress." William was holding his voice to a whisper. He signaled for the others to do the same.

"Why didn't we just tell her? Maybe they would have known what to do."

William walked closer to Orlando. "We know what to do. The more people we tell, the more people are involved. And that only increases the danger that someone will do the wrong thing. We have someone's life in our hands—that's what the note said. We have to assume that that is true until we find out otherwise."

"So what do we do? Just wait?"

"We stay in this room, and we don't let anyone in. Don't be so quick to open the door next time. And yes, we wait for Russian Roulette to contact us. What else can we do?"

No one had an answer to that. And so the boys waited. The evening dragged on forever. William wired and froze the documents, and after the lights were turned off, he did his little belly crawl and dropped the papers into the snow. When he came back, the boys were sitting on the beds.

"Did it work?" Bilbo asked.

"I don't know. It was too dark to tell. We won't know until morning. So let's just go to sleep. There's no point in sitting around worrying."

And so they went to bed. But Nutty knew that no one went to sleep. No one moved, not even to roll over, and the breathing was tight, not long and smooth. Even after an hour Nutty felt nowhere near falling asleep.

And then he heard something. At first he tried to tell himself it was nothing—just the normal sounds in a building at night. But it was too distinctive, too near. Something—or someone—was tapping on the glass doors. But that wasn't possible. The room was on the third floor. No one could be out there. There were no trees, no electric lines, nothing.

The others had heard it, too. Nutty felt how

rigid they had all become. And then he heard movement as one of them twisted to have a look. "What is it?" Nutty whispered.

"I don't know. I think it's on the balcony." This was Bilbo's voice.

"Don't get rattled," William said, in a reasonably calm voice. "There's probably some simple explanation. I'll have a look."

The room was too dark for Nutty to see William, but he heard him get up and move away. And then his vague silhouette was apparent by the doors. The tapping sound had stopped, although Nutty wasn't exactly sure when.

William stayed by the doors for a long time, and all the while the boys kept their silence. Nutty felt as though something had taken hold of him and was squeezing the breath from him.

And then William simply turned and walked back.

"What was it?" Orlando said. "Could you see anything?"

"No, I couldn't. I don't know what it was. Maybe wind or . . . something."

Nutty didn't like it when William, of all people, was baffled. "What wind?" he said.

"Well, I don't know. But nothing was out there. I don't think we're in any danger."

William got back in bed. The short, tight breaths continued for quite some time. And then the tapping began again. It was firm, steady, almost a knocking sound. And it was clearly out there on that balcony.

Chapter 4

R and R

William got up again; the tapping stopped again; he found nothing again. And then it all happened a third time. By this time the boys were sitting up in the dark, peering toward the doors, unable to see.

And then there was nothing. Ten minutes went by. Fifteen. And they heard not another sound. "Just try to sleep," William finally said. "I have some thoughts about what it might have been, but I'm not at all sure. Let's just hope it was something in the heating system, or maybe—"

"William," Orlando said, "it was something knocking right on those doors, and you know it was."

"Well, it did seem to be. But noises can be deceptive in the dark, especially when a person is upset. The important thing is, no harm has been done. Let's just go to sleep. We'll all feel better when the sun comes up in the morning."

And so they tried to sleep again. Nutty did shut his eyes; he tried to force all the thoughts away. He just wanted to sleep and get these next few hours over with. He was even drifting in that direction when Orlando screamed.

It was a terrifying moment. Nutty sat up automatically, too stunned to think what had happened. It was a few seconds before he understood.

"On the wall. On the wall," Orlando was saying. He was driving himself against the headboard of his bed, as though he were trying to get as far from the opposite wall as he could.

Then Nutty saw it. It was a wild shadow, and it was flitting about on the wall, glancing off a mirror, racing about like a huge moth. It was winged, it seemed, but it was held in a circle of light, and the light darted about with it.

"What is it? What is it?" Orlando was saying, but his voice was a harsh whisper.

"Be quiet," William said. "We're all right. I think I know what's going on. It's nothing that can hurt us."

But Nutty was not so easily convinced. He had the creepy feeling that the thing was going to dart toward him at any time. He dropped down in the bed and pulled the covers over his head.

"I think we should just get out of here," Bilbo

said. He was more controlled than Orlando, but Nutty could hear the fear in his voice.

"Yeah, come on," Orlando said. "Let's run down to the Ashes' room."

"No," William said, firmly. And then he whispered. "Just let them have their fun."

And then it was gone. Nutty didn't see it disappear; he was still hiding his head. But he heard William say, "Okay, they've stopped."

"What do you mean, 'they'?" Nutty said. "What are you talking about, William?" He sat up again.

"I'm talking about the person or persons in the next room. They're trying to scare us out of here."

Nutty tried to think whether this was true. He wasn't sure he understood what William meant.

"Next room?" Orlando said. "That thing was right on that wall."

"Yes, the shadow." William was whispering very softly now. "But the flashlight was not in the room."

Nutty thought that one over. And suddenly that did seem to be what he had seen. It could have been a beam from a flashlight with some sort of cut-out silhouette creating the shadow.

"It came from the balcony," William said. "I could see the light passing through the glass."

Nutty looked instinctively at the balcony again.

He still saw nothing in the dark. But the thought that someone was out there was anything but reassuring.

Orlando was thinking the same thing. "Someone's out there?" he said, and his voice pinched off.

"Not exactly," William whispered, and he was in control now. "Our balcony connects to another one. There's a wall between the two, but it would not be hard to reach around it with a flashlight and aim it at that wall. It would also be easy enough to reach around with a broom or a ski pole, or almost anything, and tap at those doors."

"Who do you think it is?" Bilbo said.

William considered for a time, and the room fell silent. "I've been thinking about that. It's someone who wants to scare us, probably to make us run for it and leave the room. That means they probably want to get in without dealing with us face to face. The logical conclusion is that it's someone who wants to come in and search for the documents."

"But if we stay," Nutty said, "they may decide they do have to deal with us."

"I know. That's a possibility. But if we run for it tonight, and they find nothing in the room, we will be their next target. As things stand, it's the room they want and not us."

"Why don't we just call the police, William? They're the ones who can handle this."

"I've thought that a thousand times tonight. But I still see the same dilemma. I keep wondering who Russian Roulette is. He put his faith in us. He says we must not show the papers to anyone. What if it really does mean his life?"

"Maybe he's a crook or spy or something."

"Maybe he's not."

There was no answer to that. For a time the boys said nothing. Finally William said, "Maybe they've given up for the night. Maybe they'll try to break in once we leave in the morning to go skiing. Let's just wait out the night, sleep if we can, and then try to find Russian Roulette tomorrow."

The boys thought about that, and then Bilbo said, "But William, you said yourself that if they search the room and find nothing, they'll come after us."

"I know. But not out on the slopes, I wouldn't think. Not any place where people are around. And besides, Russian Roulette will be in big danger if he tries to come to our room. We need to get outside and give him a chance to get to us."

"How will he know who we are? How will he find us?"

"I'm not sure. But I'm working on it. Go ahead and sleep. I need to do some thinking. By morning I should have something." And then William chuckled, in that old man's way of his. "Actually, fellows, this is rather exciting if you put it all in the right perspective."

"Oh, brother," Orlando said, and he dropped down on his bed.

Nothing more happened that night, and by morning William did have a plan. The boys got dressed, had breakfast, and headed for the slopes. William left a message at the front desk for anyone who might ask for them: "We're ready for R and R. We're skiing at Big Mama."

"I don't understand," Nutty whispered, as they walked out of the lodge. "How will he locate us? There'll be hundreds of people out there on Big Mama."

"There's a message board—a chalk board— right next to the lift line. You saw it yesterday, didn't you?"

"Yeah. Sure."

"We'll leave another message there. I'll ski with you while the beginners continue their lessons."

"Beginners?" Orlando said. "So what are you?"

"I read the whole book," William said, "not just the first chapter." He was kidding, of course, but the truth was, he was ready for a more challenging hill. He could manage Big Mama. Bilbo and Orlando could not.

And so they split up at the base of Big Mama,

39

and William scratched a note on the chalkboard: "RR: Leave message." Then William stepped into the lift line.

"Hold your poles with the inside hand," Nutty said, "and turn toward the chair with—"

"I know. I read about that. And I've watched the others. I can manage."

And manage he did. First time up, they got off at the mid-hill point, in order not to have to ski the steepest part at the top of the run, but William snow-plowed his way down very nicely. He never got up much speed, never took any chances, but he made nice round turns, kept in control, and made it to the bottom without a single fall.

The next time up, they went to the top. William struggled a little more with the steep part, even fell a couple of times, but he was soon doing very well— better than Nutty had done the whole week of his first skiing trip.

But Nutty didn't care about that. What he wanted most was to get in touch with this Russian Roulette and get the whole thing over with. Skiing really wasn't any fun with his mind full of everything that had happened all night.

But there was no message when they came down, nor was there the next time. Nutty was start-ing to think the whole plan had failed. Then they got to the bottom the fourth time and found an answer.

Scrawled beneath their note were the tiny words: "ticket booth, ASAP."

"Come on. Let's go," Nutty said. He looked over at the booth and saw a few people there. One man, not on skis but wearing a brown parka, was looking in their direction.

"Wait. Stay in line."

"No. Come on, William. It says as soon as possible."

"Don't look back," William whispered, "and don't act like you even noticed anything on the board. I think a couple of guys are following us."

"What? Why didn't you say so before?"

"Because I'm still not sure. But they came down behind us on our last two runs, and they stopped every time we did."

"What do they look like?"

"They're both kind of tall. One has a red parka on, and the other one is all in black. They both have ski masks on, even though it's not really all that cold this morning."

Nutty placed them now. He had seen them, just hadn't given them any thought. He nodded and then said, "They've been coming off the top. Let's get off at the mid-hill station. We can get back quicker—and we'll also get a better idea of whether they're following us."

"Good idea," William said. And then he added,

as though he couldn't resist, "I had already thought of that."

And so they did get off at mid-hill, and they set off as quickly as they could. But the men got off, too. There was nothing to do but ski as fast as possible, try to get down in time to say something to Russian Roulette, maybe arrange another place to meet.

But if William was good for a beginner, he was not fast. His slow progress was frustrating, and Nutty finally pulled up and waited. "That's right," William said, between puffs, as he approached Nutty. "We can't outski them. They're catching up. Let's stand here and talk, force them to pass us up or else wait us out." He had plowed his way to a rather awkward stop. "If they keep waiting, we know they're following us."

The men soon appeared, skiing rather fast. They seemed confused for a moment when they saw the boys stopped on the hill. They skied on by, but not long after, one spoke to the other, and they both pulled up.

"Well, they outfoxed us on that one," William said. "Now we have to ski past them—or just stand here."

"Let's just wait 'em out. It will start to get obvious."

"Yes. But they can just ski to the bottom and

wait, right where we want to make our contact." Nutty nodded, granting the point, and William kept thinking. "Let's go ahead. Ski past them, and then I'll take a fall right by them, in front of them if I can. But you keep going, as if you didn't notice. And ski as hard as you can. Try to get there far enough ahead to get to our man. Tell him to meet us some-where—anywhere. You know the area."

And so they set off. William waited until the two skiers were not far behind, and he made a fine fall. Orlando couldn't have done better. The men pulled up, avoiding William and probably assuming that Nutty would stop as well.

But Nutty was shooting the hill for all he was worth, just flat out and straight down the hill, not glancing back at all. He knew he had a good start on the men, and they couldn't pursue too hard without being obvious.

There was only one problem. From some dis-tance Nutty could see the ticket booth. The man with the brown parka was gone.

Chapter 5

Contact

Nutty waited by the booth until William made it down the hill. And then the two of them waited there until the two masked skiers, not to seem overly conspicuous, were forced to get on the chair lift.

"Well, at least they're gone for now," Nutty said. "What do we do?"

"I don't know. I'm thinking."

And Nutty let him think. He had learned not to bother William when he needed to concentrate.

Finally William said, "Something scared Russian Roulette away. Maybe he recognized the guys following us. Maybe he just didn't dare stand there any longer. In any case, the only place he knows to watch for us is here. I don't see how we can do anything but keep skiing. But let's be as unpredictable as possible and try to keep those guys off our trail."

"They'll be getting off at mid-hill, trying to get back down fast, I suspect. Let's head for the top."

"Yes, and then maybe rest at the upper lodge for a few minutes. That might confuse them."

"It might also rest your legs." Nutty smiled.

"Yes, exactly. This skiing is rather taxing, isn't it?"

Nutty laughed, but William didn't. He was not kidding. And he was also still thinking. Nutty could see that look in his eyes.

So the boys rested at the top for a few minutes, and then they skied back. When they saw the man in black and the one in the red parka down the hill in front of them, they stopped and waited for quite some time. All the same, they spotted them again at the bottom of the run. And from that time on, it was a constant game of cat and mouse.

But it was a game without a winner. No further messages appeared, no man in a brown parka showed up. Nothing happened.

In the afternoon, Bilbo and Orlando were turned loose for free skiing. They skied the bottom half of Big Mama and did fairly well. Or at least Bilbo did. Orlando was improving, but he was still floundering around. The worst part was, he kept trying to pick up his speed and look like a star, rather than playing things carefully as William did. Just when he would start to do pretty well, suddenly he would go out of control, and it was the "goose on ice" act all over again.

He rode up on the chairlift with Nutty a couple of times, and he always had some theory about his problems. "You know Nutty, I think I'm probably a better skier than I look."

"What?"

"Well, you know—some guys have a really good looking baseball swing, but they strike out all the time anyway. Other guys look a little wrong, but they hit the ball."

"Oh, I see. So you're good, you just look like you're falling all over the place?"

"Right. That's well put. I like that. I may be the best guy up here. Sure, a lot of guys look fancy and everything, but that's just appearance. When it comes to real, down-to-earth skiing, I doubt anyone can stay with me."

"Maybe not down-to-earth, but you're definitely down-to-snow a lot."

"That's a cheap shot, Nutty. I don't see why you have to . . ."

Nutty was laughing, but he was already tuning Orlando out. Under normal conditions, he would have had plenty to say, but today his mind just kept turning away from skiing. He kept twisting to look down the hill, watching for the man in the brown parka.

But the skiing continued, and no contact was made. The boys finally packed it in for the day and went back to their lodge. At least the room seemed all right—no sign that anyone had been there.

At dinner Bilbo told the guys, "Let's just have a good time tonight. Maybe those guys have given up. I didn't even see the ones with the masks the last hour or so."

"They were still around," William said. "They stayed closer to me and to Nutty than to you other guys. All the same, I think you're exactly right. It will serve no purpose to let ourselves get overly nervous. We need a good night's rest. We have no way to contact Russian Roulette; he'll have to find a way to contact us."

"I agree about resting," Orlando said. "Man, I'm wiped out."

"I guess doing that goose step on skis really takes it out of you, huh?"

"Nutty, if you think that's witty or something, check my lips. Do you see any upturned corners? Do you see any teeth showing?"

"Orlando, you sound grouchy. What's the matter?" It was Mrs. Ash. She had come up behind Orlando while he was talking.

Orlando turned around. "I'm not grouchy. It's just that people think they're funny when they're not."

"I guess things didn't go much better today."

"Hey, they went fine. I'm getting the hang of it now. As soon as I look as good as I really am, everyone will be able to see that I'm actually great at this."

"Would you run that one by me again?" But Orlando didn't bother, and Mrs. Ash looked around at the other boys. "Hey, what's with you guys?" she said. "You aren't being much a part of the group. You eat over here by yourselves; you ski by yourselves. The rest of the group has hardly seen you. You know, Nutty, that's not showing a lot of leadership."

"Oh. Well, I'll have to do better. There have been a few things happening that have . . . sort of been on my mind."

"What's the trouble? I've noticed that you all seem to be awfully serious?"

But it was William who answered. "No trouble," he said. "Nothing like that. I think this high elevation has gotten to us. We've all been rather tired."

"Now that I can understand. But it's the skiing, not the elevation, that's wearing me out. I'm ready for bed right now."

"Yes, yes. Exactly. We were just saying the same thing."

And so the boys got up and headed back upstairs. They even lived up to their promise. Twenty minutes after they got upstairs, Orlando and Bilbo were sound asleep. Nutty took his time in the shower, but once out, he was about to crash, too. And then someone knocked on the door.

William was sitting in a chair, reading a newspaper. He looked up. But Nutty was closer to the door. "Ask who it is," William said.

"Yes? Who is it?" Nutty didn't know what he expected, but he felt his chest get tight.

"I wasn't able to reach you today," someone said. "Did you get enough rest and relaxation?" It was a man with a deep voice, and he spoke low and quickly.

"It's him," Nutty said, and he opened the door. At the same time, William was telling Nutty to wait, but it was too late now. A man was stepping inside— a big man with a dark shadow of a beard and thick eyebrows.

Nutty tried to decide whether it was the man in the brown parka, but he couldn't tell. This man seemed a little larger, maybe heavier, but Nutty wasn't sure. The man was not wearing ski clothes. He had on an overcoat, buttoned up, and a dressy looking hat. He seemed surprisingly calm. And yet, when he took the hat off, his hair was matted and sweaty.

"Thank you," he said, and he wiped his forehead with his hand. "I've been waiting for the right moment. I appreciate what you've done. If you will give me the papers, I must get out of here immediately."

Something wasn't right. Nutty felt uneasy. He glanced around at William, and at the same time saw that Bilbo and Orlando were both sitting up, seemingly stunned by the sudden awakening.

"Uh—we don't have the papers in the room," Nutty said. He gave William another look. He wasn't sure where to go from there.

William stood up and walked closer to the man. "We hid the documents," he said. "They are outside the room. How do we know that you are the person who should receive them?"

"I gave you the code name," he said. "No one else knows it."

"What code name?"

"R and R." There was something grim in the man's eyes, the intent way he stared. It was almost as though he were threatening, not pleading.

"R and R are the correct letters. But that is not the code name."

The man hesitated, glanced over at the other

two boys, and then he slid his hand into his coat pocket. "I have no time to fool with you," he said. "I have a gun in this pocket. You will give me the papers now, or I'll use it."

The man did not seem desperate; he seemed resolved. Nutty did not doubt that he meant what he said. And the thought that a gun was pointed at him was terrifying. He edged back a little, wishing there were somewhere to run.

"Tell him where we hid 'em," Orlando said. "Just tell him, William."

Chapter 6

Snow Job

"That's right, William," the man said. "Tell me now."

William, however, stood his ground. Nutty could see that the wheels in his head were turning fast. But Nutty couldn't stand this, and he was about to tell the man where the papers were when Orlando beat him to it.

"I'll tell you where they are. We froze them and then we—"

"Hid them somewhere," William finished his sentence. "And as long as we are the ones who know where they are, and you don't, you would not be wise to do anything to us."

Orlando slid off the bed and stood next to William. "Let's just tell him. It's not our business."

But William kept looking at the man and not at Orlando. "If we were to tell you, we might be in greater danger. What guarantee do we have that we'll be set free once you have the documents?"

"You only have one guarantee. If you don't tell me where they are in the next five seconds, I'll start shooting."

"Tell him, William," Bilbo said.

But William said, "But you know as well as I do that you won't do that. The noise would bring a crowd very quickly, and you would never get out of here. Or if you did, you wouldn't have the documents." William glanced around. "Don't you see, guys—our best protection is keeping our mouths shut."

The man stood still for a moment, watching William, obviously considering. And then without warning, he stepped forward and grabbed Orlando. He pushed forward, carrying Orlando with him, and he headed directly for the glass doors to the balcony.

"Okay, I'll tell you. I'll tell you," Orlando was saying.

"All right. Do it now, or you go off this balcony."

"No, Orlando," William said. "He's bluffing."

The man turned around, and he had Orlando locked around the chest with one arm. He pulled the other hand from his coat and pointed it at William. "Son, you have a very big mouth. And you're going to get yourself and your friends killed. Talk now, or I throw this kid off. Then you're next. By the time I chuck three of you down, I can guarantee the last one will tell me what I need to know."

"There are people around down there. You can't throw kids off here without anyone noticing. You'll never get away with it."

"It's dark out there. I'll take my chances. Are you ready to take yours?"

"William, we've got to tell him," Nutty said, and he was getting ready to talk whether William agreed or not.

"All right. I'll tell you this much. They're in a snow bank. But you would never find them without our help."

"That's right. That's true," Orlando said, and he sounded desperate. "We'll show you the place."

"No good, boys," the man said. "We followed you from the moment you left the room this morning. You didn't have any papers with you, and you didn't go dig in any snowbank. Those papers have got to be in this room, but I don't have time to search for them. You're just going to tell me where they are."

"But he's telling the truth," Nutty said. "We can take you to them."

The man stepped back, dragging Orlando with him, and he unlatched the glass door and slid it back.

Poor Orlando was mumbling something about dropping the documents, but the man was paying no attention. He took one step outside and then spoke through the door. "Three seconds, boys—or this kid goes over."

"Okay, okay," William said, and he strode toward the doors. "Let me show you what we did." William got to the doors, with the man still standing back toward the rail. But then he put his hand on the sliding door. "If I slide this shut and lock it," he said very calmly, "you would be caught out there."

"And your friend goes off the edge."

"What good would that do you? You would still be locked out there."

Nutty was horrified. William couldn't take a chance like that. Nutty started toward the door. He would show the man exactly where the documents were. But at that moment the man stepped forward and reached around the door to grab William. And William was ready. He slammed the door hard, catching the man's arm just below the shoulder and pinning him against the door frame.

"Jump, Orlando. Jump into the snow drift," William yelled.

Orlando took no time to think. He was over the rail and gone before the man could pull loose to grab him. And when he did pull loose, William slammed the door and locked it.

"Run," William shouted. "Get out of here."

Bilbo and Nutty needed no more prompting. They beat William to the door. But they slowed in the hallway and looked around at William. "Keep going," he said. "Downstairs. We need to get help."

And so the boys went down the stairs flying, Nutty in his robe and Bilbo in his pajamas. When they hit the lobby, Nutty started yelling to the desk clerk. "There's a man upstairs. He tried to kill us."

But Nutty was yelling so wildly that the clerk just stared at him. William spotted a security man across the lobby. He had been near the front doors, but he spun around when Nutty yelled. "Come with us," William said, forcefully but rather calmly. "A man entered our room and threatened us with a gun. He's locked on our balcony."

And then William stopped, as though stunned by some realization. "No, he isn't. He must have jumped by now. Come outside."

The security man looked confused, even skeptical. But William headed for the front doors. And at the same moment Orlando came through them. He was in his faded old Superman pajamas. The snow was clinging to the fuzzy texture, so that he looked like some abominable snowman, and he had snow packed in his hair. The look on his face was wild. "William, you could have killed me," he said.

"Did the man jump?"

"Yeah. Almost on top of me."

"Where is he now?"

"Out there in the snow. I think he broke something."

The guard followed the boys out, and they found the injured man. He was up now, but stunned. He said he had landed with his arm under him, and he thought he had broken some ribs. But the guy was amazingly calm.

"Come on inside," the guard said. "I don't understand what's going on here."

"I hope you've called the police," the man said. Nutty almost dropped over. What was the guy thinking about?

"Not yet. But I will."

"Good. I don't know what kind of story these boys have told you, but the truth is, they locked me outside on their balcony. My only escape was to jump."

"Wait a minute," Nutty said. "We only did that because he threatened us with a gun."

The guard looked confused. He looked at the man as if to see whether he believed the story. But the man shrugged and said, "I have no gun. That's the most outrageous story I've ever heard."

"Uh . . ." The guard really seemed perplexed now. "Let's go inside. I'm going to let the police sort this one out."

HEARST FREE LIBRARY
ANACONDA, MONTANA

Chapter 7

Who Is Who?

And so everyone went inside. Orlando was sitting in the lobby. Someone, probably the desk clerk, had found him a blanket, but he was still shivering, and his bare feet, sticking out from under the blanket, were flushed red.

The security guard, who was just a young guy —red headed and freckled and innocent looking— told the desk clerk to call the Salt Lake City police. "Now everyone sit down," he said, when he turned around. "It's going to take a little while for them to get up here. In the meantime, I don't want anyone going anywhere."

"Young man, I can explain all of this," the man said.

"That's fine. Explain all you want, but sit down. And when the police get here, you'll have to explain again."

"Well, maybe all that's not necessary. I was angry with the boys at first, but now that I think about it, this all may have been a silly misunderstanding."

"Well, good. If we don't have to—"

But William said, "Please just wait for the police. This man claimed to have a gun, whether he had one or not. He threatened our lives. He is after some documents that were left in our room by the man who stayed there before—the man who disappeared. I believe you know about that."

But the man began to laugh. "These boys must watch too much television. Or something must have spooked them. There's a simple explanation for all this."

"Let's hear it," the guard said. He seemed to be trying to make his voice lower and more authoritative than it normally was.

"All right. My name is Spencer—Albert Spencer—I'm staying in the room right next to these boys. I was hoping to get to bed very early tonight. I need the rest." He put his hand to his side and grimaced in pain. "I doubt I'll get much now."

"We'll have someone look at that."

"I don't think it's necessary. It's not as bad as I thought at first."

The guard shrugged, as if to say, "Suit yourself."

"In any case, the boys were making a great deal

59

of noise over there. I didn't want to say too much—I was young once myself—but they just weren't quieting down. So I decided to go over and ask them to hold it down a little."

William was sitting next to Mr. Spencer, listening carefully to his every word. "Wait a minute," he said at this point, "Do you always put on a coat and hat to come next door?" But then he looked up at the guard, who was standing in front of Mr. Spencer. "I think you should wait for the police," William said.

But Mr. Spencer said, "Oh, I can explain that. I went downstairs and walked outside for a few minutes, just to get a little air before I was going to go to bed. As I came upstairs, I heard the boys really running wild. That's when I decided to stop at their door and request they quiet down."

"Okay," the security man said, "so then what happened?"

"Well, the boys opened the door and let me come in, but when I asked them to quiet down, they became quite rude, said they had paid for their room and it was none of my business what they did in it."

"Oh, man, he's nuts," Orlando said. "He's lying like crazy."

"You see," Mr. Spencer said. "That's the kind of boys we're dealing with here. And if you think that's bad, you should have heard the kind of language they used upstairs. I'm not usually one to lose my temper, but I did get upset. I gave them a pretty strong warning. But of course, this business about the gun is just pure nonsense. You can search me and see that I have no weapon of any sort."

Bilbo had sat down on a chair further back in the lobby. "We did not make any noise," he said. "We did not call him any names. Not one thing he has said is true. And don't start believing him just because he's an adult and we're kids."

"Just let me explain what happened," Mr. Spencer said. "Then the boys can tell their side of it, if they wish." The security guard nodded. "When I came into the room, I noticed that the sliding doors to the balcony were wide open. The boys had been out there earlier. I had heard them. I don't know whether they had been dropping things on people, or what they had been up to, but I told them to shut the doors and stay inside—that the noise they made out there came right into my room. They told me they would not shut the doors until they darn well pleased—except, of course, they used much stronger words."

"Lies, nothing but lies," Orlando was muttering. "The guy said he wanted those papers or he'd kill us."

But Spencer ignored all this and continued. "I walked over to slide the open door shut and this fellow here—the little one with the blanket around him

61

—charged at me like he was crazy. He got in the doorway and blocked my way and told me to keep my hands off the door and to get out of their room. By that time I was provoked, and I just reached out and grabbed him. My intent was to pull him back in the room, but the little devil fought like a wild cat, and then this other one—this little guy who thinks he's some sort of genius—ran up and slammed the door right on my shoulder. And I mean, he really got me. He had me pinned. Well, I was more out than in, so I pulled free and was outside and so was the boy who had been fighting me."

"That part's true," Nutty said, "but that's only because—"

"Just let him finish," the guard said.

"Yes, please." Mr. Spencer rubbed his hand along his ribs again. "Well, the next thing I know, the little plump one slams the door and locks it and starts yelling to the other one to jump into the snow-bank below. He acted like he thought I was going to try to hurt them. And maybe I did look like I was that mad. I can see where the boys might have thought I was out to do something like that when I grabbed the one. But I just wanted to pull him out of the doorway."

Orlando was going nuts. "He held me and said he had a gun in his pocket, and he said he was going to throw me off the balcony. Honest. He's lying every time he opens his mouth."

Spencer rolled his eyes, and then he said. "Well, sir, I think you can see that we're not exactly dealing with a troop of Boy Scouts here. These kids know how to tell a story."

"So why did you jump?" the guard said.

"Well, that was my only escape. The boy had locked the door, and then he said he was going to leave me out there until he went down to get you. 'I'm going to tell him you came in our room and threatened us,' he said. By then, I was just mad enough not to let them get away with that one. I took a look down and decided I could jump as well as the boy had. I wanted to get to you before the boys did—and give my side of the story. Unfortunately, I guess I'm not quite so agile as I thought." He chuckled. "I don't think I'll be doing any skiing tomorrow."

"No, sir, I guess not."

"All the same, I'm willing to let the whole thing drop. If the boys will promise to be quiet, I'm willing to—"

"Excuse me," William said. The guard looked at him. "I can see that you are tending to believe this story. Just let me say one more time that it is a total fabrication on his part. Consider a few things: Did anyone complain about noise or about our dropping things off the balcony? Did you see Mr. Spencer come downstairs, walk out, and then walk back in? When he got to our room, he was heated and sweaty. I don't believe he had been outside. Would I really ask my friend to jump off the balcony unless I thought he was in very serious danger? Would Mr. Spencer— if that is his name—really jump, just to get to you first? And finally, if you will check with Mrs. Ash, one of our leaders, who has been right down the hall from us, she will verify that we have not been noisy, but rather, very quiet, and that we are never abusive or profane."

The guard took a long look at William, as though he were thinking, "Are you really a kid?" But he only said, "Look, everyone just sit tight. It ain't my job to decide who did what. I'm just glad the police are going to have to take care of this one."

And so wait they did. It was almost another thirty minutes before the police arrived. The guard did ask the clerk to come up with some more blankets, which helped, but Nutty felt rather silly sitting there in the lobby in his pajamas. Fortunately, none of the kids in their group happened to come by, but those people who did walk through the lobby gave the boys some strange looks.

At the same time, there was a much bigger concern. Would the police believe Spencer—or whatever the guy's name was? If they did, would they just let him go? And if they did that, what would happen next? Nutty made up his mind that he was going to make an all-out plea to the police.

But as it turned out, the police had their own problems deciding whom to believe. They took Mr. Spencer away from the boys, into another room, and they heard his story. Then they brought in the boys. William did most of the talking, and he did an excellent job.

But the policemen were not any more willing to decide who was telling the truth than the night guard had been. They did check to see whether it was true that the previous guest in the boys' room had disappeared. But when they asked William what had happened to the documents, William hedged. "We threw them away," he said. "We didn't want them in our possession. We thought that would be too dangerous."

Had it been up to Nutty, he would have told the whole story. What William said was a sort of half-truth, and Nutty did not exactly understand why William kept holding back.

"Well, I'll tell you what," one of the policemen finally said. "This all sounds a little crazy to me— like some spy story on TV. But I'm not about to take a chance on it. We've gotta take this Spencer guy down to the hospital anyway, so we'll keep an eye on him. In the meantime, you boys will be confined to your room, and I'm going to have this security fellow sit right outside. That's so you kids don't go out— and I guess so no one comes in. Do you understand that?"

"Will you contact the officers who were searching for the man who disappeared?" William said. "I think they would believe us."

"Well, sure I'll contact them. That's just exactly what I intend to do. But if Mr. Spencer is telling the truth, you boys are in a bunch of trouble. And right now, his story sounds a lot more likely than yours does. I'll have to tell you that."

That was that. The boys were sent upstairs, and the guard was placed at their door. The frustration was terrible. It was good to know that Spencer was gone and that a guard was outside, but there was no telling how long that would last.

The boys didn't even try to sleep now. They just sat on the beds and talked, mainly about the account that Spencer had given. "It was so stupid," Orlando kept saying. "How could anyone believe that kind of stuff?"

"Well, he was a smooth customer," William said. "He knew what he was doing. He sounded confident, and he knew that people will tend to believe adults over kids."

Nutty got up and strolled across the room. That kind of thing was so irritating. "So how can we make them believe us?" he said.

"Well, we just have to rely on the facts. I think if we—"

"Hey, wait a minute." It was Nutty, and he was standing at the glass doors, staring.

"What's the matter?"

"This door. We left it shut and locked. Spencer was out there."

"Yes, of course," William said, and he walked over to the doors. The other boys followed.

But they all just stood and stared at what they saw. The door was unlocked, and it was open just a crack.

"Someone's been in here," Orlando said. "While we were gone."

William nodded, and then he said, "You didn't think Spencer was the only person we had to fear, did you?"

Chapter 8

Who Else?

"That's right, William. Spencer said, 'We followed you this morning.' "

"Yes, and I suspect his partner was not far away; probably next door. When we ran out, he must have come in."

"Did we leave the door to the room open?"

"I doubt that it matters. They're probably people who know how to get through closed doors very quickly."

"Who are they?" Orlando said. "Are they spies or crooks or what?"

"I don't know, Orlando. But they are definitely not amateurs."

The boys walked back to the beds and sat down, but they had not had much time to discuss matters when a knock came at the door. "Boys, I'm coming in," someone said.

For an instant Nutty felt panic well up in him again, and then he realized that the voice was the guard's.

Orlando was not quite so quick to recognize the voice and took a mad dash to who-knows-where before William called him back. The guard was not alone when he came in. A rather tall man in a suit was with him. He had a top coat draped over his arm and a hat in his hand. Nutty noticed that his eyes were red and bloodshot, and that he hadn't shaved since probably early that morning.

"Hello, boys," the man said. "I'm Detective Healey, from the Salt Lake City Police Department. I want to ask you a few questions."

"Could I see your badge?" William said.

This sort of embarrassed Nutty, but he knew why William was being careful. Healey pulled out a wallet and dropped it open, revealing a badge. William nodded.

"Boys, I've heard your story, and frankly, it doesn't sound to me like something you would make up. I also know about the man who disappeared, and some of the things you told our officers fit with what we know about that."

"I'm glad somebody believes us," Orlando said.

"Well, I didn't exactly say that, but I'm inclined to. I just don't understand a couple of things. Why is it you didn't call us immediately and let us know about the documents you found?"

"I suppose we didn't think they were all that important," William said. "They were written in German, so we couldn't really figure out what they said."

"German?"

Nutty saw the surprise in the man's face, and he thought he knew what William was up to. But now Nutty was getting worried. He glanced over at Bilbo, who was looking equally concerned.

"Yes. They seemed to be plans for a rocket, or something like that. We couldn't make much sense of them. It wasn't until that Spencer guy came in here and said he wanted some papers that we realized he was talking about those things."

The detective stared at William. He seemed to be sizing the situation up, doing some quick calculating. "That doesn't fit with the story you told the officers who talked to you earlier."

"Why not?"

Again there was a long hesitation. "You told them that you made a connection between the papers and the man who had stayed in this room the day before."

"No. I never said that. It was Spencer who first helped me see the connection. When he came in here, he told me he wanted the rocket plans. That's when I first thought of them."

70

Healey looked really frustrated now. "That's nonsense," he said, and he sounded irritated. "You're changing your whole story."

"No, sir. Not that I'm aware."

Nutty looked at Orlando. He was sitting on the bed, looking at William. His eyes were round and steady, as though he were baffled by this game William was playing.

"In any case, what did you do with the documents?"

"We tore them up and flushed them down the toilet."

"I don't believe that."

"Why not?"

"It doesn't make sense. Why wouldn't you just throw them in the wastepaper basket, if you saw no importance in them?"

"Well," William said, and that sly smile of his appeared, "I like to watch bits of paper swirl around in the water and then disappear. It's just something I do for fun sometimes. Aren't there things like that you like to do, Mr. Healey? Your name is Healey, isn't it?"

The man stared at William. Nutty saw that it was a stand-off. The stare was a warning; it said things he was not ready to say out loud, not with the guard standing next to him.

"Your account makes no sense. You boys are in

very big trouble. Does anyone here want to tell the truth, or would you all like to go to jail?"

Nutty saw Orlando flinch, but he said nothing.

"You mean," William said, "that here in Utah you put children in jail?"

"It's a detention home."

"How's the food?"

Healey just stared at William. He refused to answer.

"The thing is, since we're not allowed to ski, I hate to pay so much for the food and lodging. If the detention home has decent food, that might be a good spot for us—and a lot cheaper." He turned and looked at Bilbo. "What do you think, guys?"

"All right, that's enough of your smart mouth, young man. You'll be hearing more from me." He turned and walked out.

The guard started to follow, but then he stopped and said, "I don't get you, William. You better play it straight with these guys. You're getting yourself in a real mess." He went out and shut the door.

"William, why did you do that?" Orlando said.

But William looked at Nutty. "You understand, don't you?"

"I think so. I don't think he was a real cop."

"That's right. How did you know?"

"I guess it was the way he reacted to some of the things you said."

"Be more specific."

But it was Bilbo who answered. "He knew the answers to your questions—the real answers—and it made him mad when you gave different ones."

"Exactly. I—" But the phone began to ring.

Nutty picked it up. A voice on the other end said, "Hello, this is Officer Granger—Salt Lake City Police. I was one of the officers who inspected your room yesterday."

"Yes, sir."

"I've talked to the two policemen who were up there this evening. They tell me your room is guarded. Is the guard still outside your door?"

"Yes, he is."

"Don't let anyone in, all right? In fact, let me talk to the guard."

"Sir?"

"Yes."

"We did let someone in already. He said he was Detective Healey—from your police department. But we don't think he was."

"What did he want?"

"To ask us questions. And he wanted the documents we found."

"You didn't give them to him, did you?"

"No, we didn't."

There was a long pause, and then the officer said, "Son, we have no Detective Healey. You must

73

not let anyone else in. I've done some checking to-night on this Spencer guy. That's not his name. I don't know much about him yet, but I know he's connected to people who are very dangerous."

Nutty nodded, forgetting to say anything.

"Where are the documents, son?"

"They're . . . uh. We got rid of them. We don't have them anymore."

"Where did you put them?"

Nutty held his breath, and he looked at William, who was vigorously shaking his head. "I can't tell you that, sir. I just don't have any way to know who you are for sure. You might be . . . anyone."

"But you do know where the documents are?"

"I didn't say that. I just said we got rid of them."

"All right. That's fine. Say the same thing to anyone else—or less. Now let me talk to the guard."

Nutty got the guard, and the guard got his in-structions not to move from the door all night, not to sleep, to get another man if necessary, but never to leave the door.

When the guard went back out, he was looking much more serious about the whole matter. The boys just sat and looked at each other.

"William, I don't know if we can trust anyone," Nutty said.

"We can't afford to, Nutty. For one thing, we

need to watch our dear friend the security guard out here."

"He's too dumb to be a fake," Orlando said.

"I tend to agree," William said. "But we can't assume anything."

"But what can we do?" Bilbo said. "Russian Roulette can't get to us either. And we can't get out to him. We can't just keep telling the police we don't know where those papers are."

"Yes, I'm well aware of that." William looked off in space for a time, apparently letting some things run through his mind. "We've got to get out of here for a while tomorrow," he said. "Some way or another."

Chapter 9

Ski Jump

By morning, William had a plan. But Orlando didn't like it.

"William, you're nuts if you think I'm jumping off that balcony again. There's no way."

William was sitting in a chair in his blue flannel pajamas, and he was bundled up besides in a terry-cloth robe. The room was quite dark, and the other three boys were still in bed. "Orlando," William said, "whisper. Don't talk so loud. And don't let your emotions rule your head." William was whispering very softly himself. "You jumped once without the slightest injury. As long as you jump straight down and land in the fluffy snow, it isn't dangerous at all. That snow drift must be fifteen feet high."

"Tell that to that Spencer guy."

"That's a different matter, Orlando. He's not as

young as we are, and he must have gotten off balance. He landed on his side, with his arm under him. We'll be much more careful."

"Maybe you will, but I won't. I've made my last sky dive for this trip."

"Orlando, that's—"

"Wait a minute, William," Bilbo said, "someone is bound to see us jumping off like that."

"Not if we do it right away. Not many people will be stirring around yet."

"That's right," Orlando said. "That's because they have some brains. I'm going back to sleep. You guys go ahead and make your death drop and give me some peace."

"Orlando, hold your voice down," William whispered. "Actually, though, that's not a bad idea. In fact, it's perfect. I was thinking that the drop will not be bad if we get over the ledge and use a towel, like a rope, to hang down a little ways. That will reduce the distance of the drop by a few feet—and make it easier. But one guy would have to pull the towel back in, or it would be spotted later on. The longer it takes the guard to realize we're gone, the better."

"Are you serious? You mean you would leave me here all by myself?"

"Yes, of course. If the guard knocked or asked how things were going, you could say that everyone wanted to sleep in. That could delay his finding we're gone for quite some time."

Orlando was thinking this over. "Wait a minute. You know how that guard is. He won't ask from outside. He'll come walking in. And I can't say that you're all three in the bathroom at the same time."

"Well, no. If that happens, just admit we're gone."

"Yeah, and then I have to stay and face the music."

"I suppose you could say that." Nutty thought he saw now what William was up to. "And I suppose there is one danger. Should the guard then run off, that would leave you here alone. And I suppose there are those around who are just waiting for a chance to get into this room. You might have to deal with that sort of thing."

Orlando sat up in bed. "Deal with what sort of thing?"

"That's hard to say, isn't it? I don't really think it's beyond them to resort to violence. Maybe a little jump into the snow wouldn't be so bad by comparison."

"I'm going first," Orlando said, and suddenly he was up and searching around for his ski pants.

"Good idea," William said. He was smiling now. "But be very quiet. I'll go last and jump without that towel. I seem to have the most padding."

"But what about that guard?" Bilbo whispered. "He might give us another hour or so, but then he's likely to come in to check on us. Or Mrs. Ash might come by."

"I know. I've thought about that. I wrote this, and I'm going to slide it under the door into the hallway, just before we leave. It should buy us some more time." The boys took turns reading the note. It said, "Orlando had a very restless night. He finally got to sleep toward morning. Please don't come in and wake him. I'll let you know when we're all up. Thank you, William."

"Why do you always say stuff like that about me?" Orlando whispered. "I—"

"Because I want people to believe me. That's why. But never mind now. Let's just get out of here."

And so the boys got ready, and they all made the leap, William going last. Orlando complained that he hurt his ankle, that it was too early in the morning, that it was too cold outside, that he needed some breakfast, that William was going to get them all killed, that skiing was a stupid sport anyway, that he never should have left home, and that Nutty never should have thought of such a stupid idea as a ski trip. You might say, he wasn't in the best of moods.

But the boys went to another lodge, got themselves some breakfast, and then picked up their rental skis just before the chair lifts were to start operating.

So far all was going well. No one seemed to be looking for them; no one seemed to be following. Now if they could just find some way to make contact with Russian Roulette.

"Leaving another note on the chalkboard might be dangerous," Nutty told William as they were approaching the Big Mama lift. "Those guys who were following us will be watching that board, too."

"I know, Nutty. But what choice do we have? If Russian Roulette is still around, it's the one place he's most likely to check. We need to make contact as soon as we can. Both the police and . . . the other guys, whoever they are, will be looking for us before long."

So all four boys got on the chair lift. And William left a note. "Rail Road crossing. Upper lodge."

"You sure he'll get that?" Orlando said.

"I spelled it as two words, and I capitalized the R's; I don't know how I could be more obvious."

"You could say, 'Hey, Russian Roulette, we're at the upper lodge,' and then sign your name to it."

"Yes, I could do that, Orlando." William rolled his eyes. "I could also have you stand here and ask everyone who comes by whether or not he's armed and dangerous."

"Hey, good idea. I'm getting tired of trying to figure out who the bad guys are. I want to see who they are and punch their lights out."

This was a good sign. Orlando was talking big again. It was sure evidence that his spirits were rising.

But after the boys took the lift to the top, the wait was anything but fun. Everyone who came by seemed to be looking at them. And there was no telling what it meant. They were watching for the man in the brown parka, but they could not really ask anyone for the code name, and chances were just as good that it was the enemy who had seen the message as that it was Russian Roulette.

After an hour Orlando was upset all over again. And he was about to drive everyone nuts. He had never been good at sitting still, but now he was unbearable. Every two minutes he asked what time it was, and then he would mumble about William's stupid plan, about the fact the was not learning how to ski sitting in a lodge, that the whole trip was a disaster.

"Look, Orlando," Nutty said. "It's not William's fault that we walked into this situation. It's just one of those things we couldn't control."

"I'm not so sure about that. You and William always seem to get into messes. I think you called ahead and said, 'Do you have a room that has recently been occupied by a disappearing person, especially one who hides important documents in drain pipes?' "

"Soften your voice," William whispered. "Do

81

you want someone to hear you?" And then in a moment, "Nutty, let's ski down. You and I can make it the fastest. Let's just check the board to see if there's any indication that Russian Roulette has gotten the word. I don't think we have much time now before someone is on our trail."

"You mean you're going to leave us here?" Orlando said.

But William looked at Bilbo. "Should anyone make contact, be very careful. Make sure that the person uses the name Russian Roulette and not just RR."

"What if he does? What if the real guy shows up? What should I do?"

"Start down the slope. Nutty and I would see you from the lift and catch up with you. If no one seemed to be following, I suppose we would take him to the documents. It would only take a few minutes to dig them out and hand them over. Once we've done that, our responsibility to him would be over."

Bilbo nodded, but then he said. "What if he's a spy or something? What if we're helping someone who stole those papers?"

"That's possible, Bilbo," William said. "It really is. It's a dilemma I've thought about constantly since we first found the papers. But he trusted the person who found them to save his life. I can't give up that trust. I hope you fellows can't either."

For once, Orlando kept his mouth shut. The boys all seemed to respect what William was standing for at the moment.

But there was no time for further consideration. Nutty and William set out. And Nutty probably skied a little faster than he should have in his eagerness to get to the bottom unnoticed. Poor William was a little shaky on his first run of the day but tried to keep as close as he could to Nutty. They had not gone far, however, when William took a forward plunge. Both skis went flying, and Nutty had to help retrieve them.

It was while William was getting his skis back on that Nutty first noticed a couple of men, both in dark blue ski outfits. They were not the two from the day before. One was quite tall and thin, and the other was a strong looking guy with big shoulders. Neither one was wearing a ski mask, but they kept their heads turned away. Nutty would have thought nothing about them except that they stopped for a long time, as long as it took William to get his skis back on.

When the two boys started out again, Nutty glanced back, and the men were now coming behind them. "Just a second," Nutty said to William, and he christied to a stop. He reached down then and adjusted one of the buckles on his boot. The two men skied on by and continued for quite some time. Nutty was about to forget about them when he saw them pull up. One glanced back up the hill.

"William," Nutty said, "those two guys—"

"I know. I noticed."

"They're not the same ones."

"You're right about that, too. I hate to think that we have that many people involved in whatever is going on."

"So what do we do?"

"The only thing we can do is ski on down, and then watch to see whether these guys stay on our trail."

By the time they were to the bottom, Nutty had almost forgotten about the chalkboard. The two skiers in blue had skied to the bottom and then stopped. They let William and Nutty get in the lift line, and then they got in a little way behind. Nutty was so conscious of them that he didn't look at the board until he was almost up to it. But then he saw. "Hey, William—"

"I know. I already read it," William whispered.

The boys' message was gone—erased—and instead was a note that read: "Train delayed. Will arrive."

There was nothing to do but get back to the upper lodge and wait. And so the boys took the lift and then skied over to the lodge.

"So what happened? Did you see anything?"

Orlando wanted to know. But Nutty and William sat down and just watched the door.

"What's going on? How come you guys look so scared?"

"Just a moment," William said, calmly, "we're not frightened exactly, we just—"

"There they are," Nutty said. The two skiers were coming through the door to the lodge.

William nodded. "All right. There's no question that they are following us. And I don't think Russian Roulette will try to get to us as long as they're around. We've got to shake them and then come back."

"How can we do that?" Nutty asked.

"Well, I have a plan. I thought of it on the way up on the lift. Let's all go. Just stick with me no matter what happens."

But Orlando was leaning forward, holding up his head with both hands. "Oh, brother," he moaned. "Not another one of William's plans."

Chapter 10

Turn About Is Fair Play

The boys were standing at the top of the Big Mama slope, looking down. "There's no way," Orlando was mumbling, sort of whining. "I'm not going down there."

"It's only steep here at the top," Nutty said. "Just take it easy and do your snowplow. Once we get down a little ways, it's not so bad."

"It's straight down, Nutty. What are you talking about? It's just like jumping off that stupid balcony again."

"Don't be silly," William said. "A fellow of your athletic ability should have no trouble at all."

"Don't try to con me, William. You've already conned me into two jumps—but I'm not going for it again."

"Maybe he and Bilbo should stay here again," Nutty said.

"I doubt that it would work. Now that those two guys know we're all together, they would probably split up and each take two of us."

"All right, let's do this," Nutty said. "William and I will start out, and if both guys follow us, Orlando, you and Bilbo take off your skis and hike back up to the lodge. But if they split, you'll have to come."

William nodded his agreement. "Yes, that would be excellent. We could use someone back at the lodge."

"I'm not skiing down, no matter what," Orlando said.

"Sooner or later, you'll have to. Unless you want to spend the rest of your life up here."

"I'll hike down next summer," Orlando muttered. "And then I'll never put skis on my feet again. It's the stupidest sport ever invented. It's dangerous —do you know that? A guy could really hurt himself."

"Yes, that's correct," William said. "A person can also find out what he's made of. Those with little or no courage should stay away from the sport."

"I told you not to try to con me, William." Orlando stood quietly for a moment, and then he added, "I'm not scared. I have plenty of courage. But you don't have to jump off a cliff to prove you have courage."

"It's not a cliff, Orlando. It's just—"

"Never mind," William said. "We must stop wasting time. Nutty and I will start out. If only one follows, you must follow. Bilbo, you come. I don't think Orlando will stay here by himself."

Bilbo nodded, but he looked almost as frightened as Orlando, even though he didn't say so.

Nutty pushed off, and he took the slope slowly, trying to show Orlando that it really wasn't so bad. William followed, traversing the steep hill rather than heading directly down.

The men in blue had stayed at the top, standing well away from Bilbo and Orlando. But now they hesitated, seeming not to know what to do. They waited for some time, and gradually Nutty and William were well down the hill. And then one of them took off, skiing quite rapidly, obviously trying to catch up. But the other one stayed at the top.

By now Nutty had pulled up to let William catch him, but also to check the hill. He saw only one blue figure at the top, and then he saw the other man coming down the run. He could also see that Bilbo was doing some hard talking with Orlando.

And then Orlando eased off the top, angling across the hill. His legs were wide apart, the skis in a wedge, and he seemed anything but stable as he wobbled along. All the same, he did all right until he ran out of room and had to turn. As the turn took him downhill, he picked up speed and suddenly lost everything. In a moment he was tumbling downward, his skis flying over him.

Bilbo was getting along fairly well. He managed to get to Orlando and help him up. But it was some time before Orlando had his skis back on and could begin all over. Nutty almost went crazy, waiting, aware that the men in blue were waiting, too.

Eventually Orlando got himself off the steepest part of the slope, and he began to make better progress. True, he fell several more times, but he didn't lose his skis again, so he was up and going much more quickly. When he finally caught up with Nutty and William, he was doing the last thing Nutty expected. He was smiling.

"Hey, that wasn't so bad," he said. "I'm getting a lot better. How did I look?"

Nutty made no comment. And William just said, "All right, then. Follow me. I'm taking the side trail that leads back to the main lodge."

"What's the plan?" Nutty said.

"Let's not take time to talk it out now. Just trust me. I know how we can lose these guys."

William pushed off, but just then a voice boomed down the hill. "Stop right there, young man."

William did stop. Nutty froze. He hadn't expected these guys to try anything out there on the ski slope. But then he heard William say, "Oh, hello, Mr. Crawford."

Nutty looked up to see Crawford skiing toward them. Further on up the hill he could see Mrs. Crawford, skiing slowly with some of the other kids from their group. They were obviously trying Big Mama for the first time.

Crawford stopped near the boys. "What in the world is going on?" he said. "I stopped by your room this morning and some security guard was sitting outside. He said you were all asleep and he was assigned to watch your room."

"Is that all he told you?" William said.

"Yes. That's all he would tell me—except that the police are involved. What have you boys been up to?"

"Nothing, really," Nutty said. "It's kind of a long story." He glanced around to see that the two men were still waiting on the hill above them. "We found something and—"

"It's nothing serious," William said. "But I'll have to admit, we played a joke on the guard. He fell asleep, so we just slipped by him. Maybe we better head back there now and let him know he doesn't have to stay there any longer."

"But what's up? Why did you need a guard?"

The other skiers were approaching now. One of the boys managed to get himself stopped and then said, "Oh, man, I made it." And then when he saw who was there, he said, "Hey, where have you guys been? We've hardly seen you. We came by your room last night, and some guy said we couldn't even talk to you. What the heck's going on?"

This was getting more complicated. And time was passing. William suddenly spoke with authority. He looked at Mr. Crawford and said, "I'm sorry, sir, but we just don't have time to explain things right now. We better get back to the lodge and get everything straightened out. I believe this trail over here will get us there."

"Now wait a minute. I—"

"I'm sorry, we do have to go. Why don't we all meet for lunch at the lodge. We'll have quite a story to tell you." William pushed off, and Nutty went right behind.

Orlando said, "I mean a real story," and he and Bilbo pushed off, too.

And so down the side trail they went. Nutty was glad in a way that Crawford hadn't pushed things any further, but he missed the momentary safety he had felt with an adult around. Maybe they should have asked Crawford to go with them. But Nutty knew what William would say about that. Mr. Crawford would want to call the police immediately, and William was still committed not to do that.

The trail was narrow, giving the three novice skiers little room to turn. The progress was slow. At first it seemed that the two skiers in blue had stopped following, but Nutty eventually spotted them. They were staying well back, clearly aware that the boys would be struggling and moving slowly.

When the boys finally reached the lodge, William told them to take off their skis and to follow him. But then Nutty saw where William was going. He was heading for the line that would get them on the tram—and the tram would take them all the way to the top of the mountain. There was no way Orlando could ski up there.

"William, wait a minute," Nutty said. "We can't—"

"No," Orlando suddenly said, and he stopped. "William, you're not getting me up there."

William stepped back, and he said, very softly, "Orlando, I don't plan to ski from up there any more than you do. Just trust me."

"I've trusted you enough. I'm staying right here."

"Orlando, those two guys are coming up behind us right now. They might love to get hold of one of us. They might want to torture the truth out of us."

"They don't have to torture me. I'll just tell 'em."

"Look, I have no time for your childish games. Just come along." William grabbed Orlando just above the elbow and found a vulnerable spot. He applied one of his death grips.

Suddenly Orlando was moving. "All right. All right. Let go, will you?"

But William kept him marching, all the while saying, "You won't have to ski down. I promise you. I have a plan." And once on the crowded tram, William whispered, "You guys follow me when we get off. Do exactly what I do."

Orlando was pushed up against a window, and he was staring out. "I don't like stuff like this," he was saying. "I'm not scared. I just don't like it. Some guys don't like closed in places. Some don't like high places. And some don't like drop-offs with snow on them. I guess I'm one of 'em. Look down there."

Nutty had to admit there was some tough skiing down below. He had skied from the top, but he had taken the easiest route down. He knew there was no way that the other guys could make it. What in the world was William up to?

It took six minutes to get to the top. William timed it. The tight-packed skiers gradually moved off, and William led his little group to the building not far away. It might have been beautiful up there,

93

if a person were not terrified out of his mind, but the wind was whipping around the building and clouds were scudding by, partially blocking the view. It was hard to relax and take in the scenery.

"It's straight down on every side," Orlando said.

"How do you know?" Nutty said, "you haven't looked."

"I saw from the tram."

"It really is pretty bad," Bilbo said, and he looked pale.

William stopped by the building. "Okay, just stand here," he said. "And don't worry about having to ski down."

"Not worry? What do you mean not worry? We're not ready for this. You're crazy to—"

"Hush, Orlando. Here they come. Nutty, act like you're adjusting your boots."

The two men headed toward them, but were suddenly surprised to see the boys waiting. They both ducked their heads and then veered off around the opposite side of the building.

"Excellent," William said. "They won't dare come back around. They'll be waiting for us on the other side."

"What good does that do us?" Bilbo said.

"Just hang on a few more seconds, and you'll see." And now Nutty understood.

"We're getting back on, aren't we?" he said.

But just then William said, "All right, come with me. He hurried back to the tram, just as the operator was about to shut the door. "Just a moment," he said.

The operator looked out. "Having second thoughts?" he said, and he grinned.

"Yes, sir. I'm afraid we overestimated our ability. I don't think we're ready for this."

"Hey, that's fine. Better to ride back down than to get yourselves hurt."

William was already walking on by the operator, and the other boys hurried on in behind him. The operator laughed at their haste, and then he shut the door. "Almost every day I have a few people turn around. Usually they don't make up their minds quite so fast though."

But the boys were paying no attention. They had gone to the windows to look out. Just as the tram began to move, a head peeked around the building. The man saw what had happened and took a quick step out. He made one wave, as though he thought of signaling the operator to stop. But then he seemed to realize it was too late and just dropped his hands to his side.

"All right," Orlando said, and he laughed. "This is the only way to ski."

Chapter 11

Downhill Racers

William was looking at his watch now, and he was doing some quick calculations. Nutty was doing some thinking of his own. "William," he said, "do you think they'll ski down or wait for the next tram?"

"I don't know. How long do you think it would take them if they ski?"

Nutty thought for a moment. "I'm not sure. They're fair skiers, but not really hot shots. I don't see how they could do it faster than half an hour. It's a long run clear from the top."

"The next tram comes in six minutes—at the same time we reach the bottom—and it takes maybe two or three to unload and start down. Then it's six more minutes down. If they take the tram and don't ski, they're better off. They would only be eight or nine minutes behind us."

"Maybe they'll take off skiing before they figure all that out," Orlando said.

"That's a very real possibility," William said, and now he was looking out the window, back toward the top of the hill, but there was no chance of seeing the men. "We can't count on it though. We need to ski our best to make it back to the Big Mama lift as quickly as we can. If we have a lot of trouble, they could catch us."

"It only takes three or four minutes to ski the road back to Big Mama," Nutty said. "And it's not steep at all."

"But if it takes us longer—say five or six minutes—and it probably will, they could end up just a few minutes behind us. We have a very narrow window of time to find Russian Roulette, if he happens to be at the lodge now."

"How will those guys know we're heading back up Big Mama?" Bilbo asked.

"They may not. But it's the most logical guess. They've probably seen our messages."

The tram was suddenly silent. Everyone was doing his own thinking. But it was Orlando who said, "What happens once they catch up to us? That guy sort of admitted they were following us when he stepped out and waved like that."

"Yes. Exactly. They may come out in the open now."

"What does that mean, William? What do you think they would do to us?"

"I have no way of knowing, of course. We just have to hope we can make quick contact and then start down the slope before they catch up."

"Maybe I ought to go ahead," Nutty said. "I could save maybe a couple of minutes."

"I know. But there's one problem with that. These fellows on our trail are not the same ones we saw yesterday. There may be others out there. I don't like the idea of separating now. At least we have some strength in our numbers."

No one needed further convincing. Again the boys were quiet as the tram slowed. It was nearing its destination. Nutty felt a tightness in his chest and a rolling sensation in his stomach. If only he could ski for those guys. Holding back to stay with them would be murder.

But the problems started before he ever got a chance to ski. Orlando tried to hurry too fast to get his skis on. His bindings wouldn't seem to work right. Twice he lifted up his foot only to have the boot pop right back off the ski. Nutty finally reached down and set the bindings correctly, so that the boot snapped in, but Orlando had dropped his poles while he was fussing with the bindings, and when he tried to bend to pick them up, his skis slid forward, and he lost his balance and fell. Nutty helped him up, all the while watching the tram, which was filling up fast and would soon be on its way. They had already lost way too much time.

"All right now, Orlando," William was saying. "Hurrying will cost you in the long run. Just ski conservatively. Do your wedge and don't get going too fast. You'll do much better that way than if you push too hard and end up falling."

Orlando seemed to pay no attention at all. As soon as he was up and had his poles in hand, he pushed off, forgot all about the wedge and just headed down the trail. It wasn't steep, but he soon had too much speed for his own good. When he did try to bring his skis into a snowplow, the tips crossed, and he went flipping head over heels. One ski stayed on, but the other one went skidding away.

William helped him get up, and Nutty got the ski, but now they had to deal with the bindings again. "I don't know why these skis do that," Orlando was mumbling. "When I try to do a snowplow, like everyone tells me to, the dumb things cross over and knock me down."

Nutty could not take much more of this. "Criminy, Orlando," he said, "it's not the skis. You have to—"

"Just listen to me," William said. "Apply your

snowplow from the beginning. Hold the tips apart, and don't get going so fast this time."

"All right. All right."

Nutty could see the tram disappearing over the first low hill. That meant the other one—the one coming down—was on its way. In less than six minutes those two guys could be down.

But Orlando did better this time. He made it along the trail without falling. It was Nutty who fell. And this he couldn't believe. He had gotten a little ahead and then looked back. As he did, one ski caught a little icy spot and got away from him. He was up quickly, but not before Orlando was saying, "Didn't you listen to William? Don't get going too fast."

"Listen, I—"

"Never mind. Never mind. Just keep going," William said.

But Orlando had outdone himself and was due for another disaster. And fate caught up with him. A faster skier was coming down the trail. He called out, "Left," and went by on that side, but the unexpected voice made Orlando jerk, and suddenly his skis were heading in opposite directions. When he went down this time, he slammed the ground awkwardly, moaned, and made no move to get up.

Nutty felt himself give up. They would never

make it to the chair lift ahead of those guys now. But William was there, close to Orlando. "Where are you hurt? Is it serious?"

Orlando groaned once, and then he said, "I'm hurt all over. That's where. So get off my back."

Nutty took a breath in relief. He wasn't hurt all that bad, or he wouldn't be so sarcastic.

William was already tugging on him. "Well, feel sorry for yourself later. You'll live—if we get going."

Orlando struggled to his feet again. And he only had one more minor accident on the way to the lift.

The lift line was actually very short, but it seemed to Nutty that it took ten minutes to get to the front of it—even though it could not have been more than two or three. All the same, he expected to see the two skiers coming down that road and appearing any second. And the lift seemed to have changed gears—it hardly seemed to move at all.

As they rose up the slope, however, William said, "Still no sign of them. But they could be closing the gap right now."

"Maybe they got too anxious and skied down."

"That's what I'm hoping."

They rode on in silence after that, looking back until they were finally too far up the slope to spot the men any longer. Then they just waited as the lift seemed to grind ahead in slow motion.

Nutty spotted the Crawfords again, with their little group. And right behind them were Mr. and Mrs. Ash and another group. No one looked up at the lift; they were all struggling too hard to get down the mountain. But Nutty felt a longing to yell out to them, to feel near them. He had no idea what would happen if those guys caught up. How had this perfectly nice ski trip turned into such a mess?

When the lift finally neared the top, Nutty could hardly sit in the chair. He wanted to jump off before it got to the actual end. But in a moment he was sliding down the little hill from the lift and heading for the upper lodge, praying that he could spot the man in the brown parka.

And then he saw something else. He christied to a stop immediately, and he waited for William. "Do you see them?" he said.

"See what?"

"Over by the lodge. It's the two guys who followed us yesterday."

William looked over and then replied, very calmly, "Oh, dear. I was afraid of something like that."

"What'll we do now? We've got guys on both sides of us."

"Yes. That is a problem." Orlando and Bilbo

were catching up now. "Don't tell the others. No use causing them worry. Let's just go in the lodge and hope our man is there."

They skied on to the lodge, took their skis off and went inside. Nutty glanced at the men, but they turned their backs, acted as if they didn't notice the boys.

Inside, William wasted no time. He walked up the stairs to the large snack bar area and in an exaggerated voice, much louder than usual, said, "It's like a railroad crossing out there. I need some R and R."

A man spun around. It was the man in the brown parka. He walked immediately to the boys.

"All right," he said. "I'm glad I finally found you. I was beginning to think—"

"Give me the code name," William said.

The man looked surprised, and for a moment Nutty had the sickening thought that he didn't know. He was not a grim-looking man, however, not someone Nutty could think of as an enemy. He was a trim-looking person, well groomed, and he was soft-spoken.

"Russian Roulette," he said. "You're right to be careful."

"We can take you to the documents," William said, "but I don't know whether—"

"I'm not concerned about that right now. I'm

worried about your safety. Have you seen anyone following you?"

"Yeah," Orlando said. "A couple of guys in blue parkas followed us all over the place."

"Where are they now?"

"We managed to shake them," Nutty said. "But they might not be too far behind us now."

Nutty saw the man's reaction. His jaw tightened and his eyes closed for a moment. "That's too bad," he said. "Those were police officers. They were looking out for you."

"Oh, dear," William said again, and for once there was some real concern in his voice.

Nutty felt his insides grip. "Those guys outside . . ." he said, but he didn't finish.

"The two men outside—one in red and one in black—have you seen them before?"

"Yes, they followed us yesterday."

"Are they cops, too?" Orlando said.

"Hardly," the man said, speaking softly. "I'm afraid we're in a pretty bad spot. I'm really sorry."

Chapter 12

Slow in the Snow

Everyone seemed to see them at the same time—
the two men coming up the stairs. And when they
reached the top, they made no pretense. They stared
directly at Russian Roulette and the four boys.

"Our best bet is to stay right here," Russian
Roulette whispered to the boys. "We're safest with
lots of people around. We need to stall until the
police catch up."

"What do they want?" Orlando said. "What's
going on anyway?"

But there was no time for discussion. The men
were walking toward the boys. They had taken their
ski masks off. As they approached, Nutty could see
that one of them—the tall one in red—was the man
who had claimed to be a detective.

"Hello," he said, calmly. "We've had a little
trouble locating all of you today, but now that we're

all together, why don't we stroll outside where we can have a little chat."

"We would prefer to stay right here where we are," William said.

It was a stand-off. The two men glanced at each other, seemed to consider. And then the tall one reached out and put a hand on Orlando's shoulder. Orlando tried to step back, but the man had him in a tight grip.

"I think this young man and I will just stroll outside alone then. The rest of you stay here, if that's what you prefer. This boy, however, is in serious danger of meeting with a skiing accident. There are some bad cliffs not far from here. A novice skier shouldn't even go near them."

Orlando began to mumble something about everything always happening to him; but William said, "If you try to take him out of here, I'll scream for help."

"Well, that's something you could do, of course." The man smiled. "But it wouldn't be wise. I have a gun in this pocket." His hand was in the pocket, and he hiked it up a little. "It has a silencer on it. Were I to shoot you, you would slump to the ground, but it would take a few minutes for people to figure out what in the world had happened. In the confusion I would take this boy with me and get away. I assume that he knows where the documents are. I only need one of you."

"I'll tell you where they are right now," Orlando said.

Now it was Russian Roulette who spoke. "I don't believe you would try that. You aren't going to shoot anyone in the middle of this crowd. That's too sloppy."

"Well, let's say, it would not be the preferred method. On the other hand, you are leaving me little choice. I will not stand here much longer. I simply can't. You, of course, can gamble that I won't shoot, but you are gambling with these boys' lives. A much better choice would be for all of us to ski down the hill, locate the documents, and put an end to this whole game we've been playing."

"I suspect we have a better chance of staying alive if we don't give you those papers," William said.

"Well, now that's not true. I actually don't like to shoot people. Once I have the documents, I'll not bother you again."

"Are we supposed to trust you on that one?"

"You really don't have a lot of choices. Go ahead and scream; see if I'm not a man of my word. Or refuse to cooperate and take a chance that I won't shoot one or two of you to 'encourage' the others to turn over the documents."

"Just take me," Russian Roulette said.

"Look, Mr. Fullmer, I have no more time for stupid talk. Take your choice now. Let's all go—or one of you start yelling for help. I want to know which one of you to shoot."

"We better go with them," Fullmer said. "These men are capable of anything. We'd be playing Russian roulette if we tried anything."

Nutty thought he knew what Fullmer was hinting. The game—the stall—was actually continuing. The policemen might not be far behind. But it was hard to tell what they had done. They might have skied off the mountain, or maybe they didn't head directly for Big Mama. If they had, they should have been there by now. If only William's plan hadn't worked so well.

In another moment Nutty knew that the plan was to stall. Fullmer said he needed to get his ski gloves, and then he took his time putting them on. And William got downstairs to the door, but then he had a terrible time with the zipper on his parka.

"Come on," the man in black said, under his breath. But William just kept saying that something was wrong with the stupid thing, until he finally had to be pushed along.

As they all walked outside, Nutty looked about for the men in blue parkas, but saw no sign of them. He took his time getting his skis on, and then he claimed to be helping Orlando, but he actually set the bindings wrong, so that Orlando had trouble snapping his boot in.

The man in the red ski outfit waited calmly for a time, and then he said, "I don't know what you expect to gain by stalling, but I'll tell you this— you're taking a big chance. I want you to ski down this slope now, and take me directly to the documents. I will not fool with you much longer."

And so they all started out toward the crest of Big Mama. They had hardly started down the run, however, when William took a bad spill, and then Nutty had a turn. In the meantime, Orlando had been down twice and so had Bilbo. Nutty knew that his own fall had been on purpose, and he was sure that William's had been, too. Orlando and Bilbo probably didn't need to fake.

But the tall man was furious. "All right," he said, and he stood before Fullmer and the boys, "I know what you're doing, and it leads me to believe that you think help is on the way. I'm not sure why you think so, but it makes me feel that we better hurry. If one of you were to fall out here and not get up, it might take some time before anyone stopped to check on you, and more time to figure out that the blood was from a bullet wound. So I'm willing to take that chance and use this gun. Now let's not have any more falling."

Nutty saw Orlando's eyes get round. "But, sir," he said, "this is only my third day of skiing—and only the second time up here. I can't help it."

"I would suggest you catch on—now. You have a wonderful incentive to improve. Let's go."

But Nutty had spotted something. The two policemen. They were on the lift, heading toward the top. They were looking down, obviously perceiving what was happening, but, of course, were not in any position to do anything. Nutty guessed it would take them another two or three minutes to reach the top, and at least that long again to catch up, even if progress was slow. But how slow did he dare go? He was not about to try any more falls.

But now everyone was moving again. Orlando was going very slowly, but he was staying up. He was doing an expert snowplow, making wide, slow turns, just the way William had started out. Bilbo was doing the same. They were getting off the steepest part of the run and progress became steady.

Nutty didn't dare glance around, but he knew the policemen were a long way from catching up. Once the seven of them reached the bottom and walked away, the police might not be able to locate them. And Nutty just could not believe that these two men would simply take the documents and leave. He hated to think what they might do.

As Nutty pondered, Orlando's luck ran out. He lost his balance, fought to stay up, but then slipped onto his side. He was up almost immediately, all the while pleading. "It was an accident. Honest. I'm going again. Really."

"Don't have any more accidents, son," the man said. "Do you understand?"

"But I can't—"

Orlando looked over to see William take a real nose dive. Nutty had no idea if it had been on purpose or not, but he caught his breath, wondering what the man would do. It was the one in black who skied over and pulled William to his feet.

"All right, you've pushed me far enough," the fellow grumbled.

"Hello, down there," someone was yelling. "Nutty, Orlando." It was a boy from their school. And now more voices were chiming in.

Nutty waved, watched the group glide by above, then glanced over at the man who had hold of William. "Friends of ours," he said.

With that William spoke in his most reasonable tone. "Sir, we're beginners. I don't know what you can expect. The extra pressure you're putting on us is only adding to the difficulty. You'll have your documents soon enough."

The one in red skied over to William. "Just get

going," he said, "and I'm telling you, this is the last time you pull that one."

"But how can you say that I'm pulling anything? I merely—"

"Get going."

"Just one moment. In case you hadn't noticed, one of my skis came off." William bent forward to grab the ski, but the other ski suddenly shot out from under him, and he took a wild fall. He ended up right across the tall man's skis.

For a moment there was a hasty struggle for William to get to his feet, with some less-than-gentle help from above. "Excuse me. Excuse me," William was saying. "I'm being terribly awkward. But you've made me so nervous I can hardly help it."

"Look, kid. You've never been nervous in your life. But you better get that way right now. I don't think you believe me yet."

If William wasn't nervous, Nutty was. All the same, he took a chance and glanced up the hill. There were two dark figures above. Maybe it was the two policemen. They were skiing hard, but they were still a long way off, and the boys were not far from the bottom of the hill now.

William was up. And he was moving again. He even took off a little faster. All the boys moved on behind him, and so did the man in black. The other one let everyone else go ahead before he started out. They hadn't gone far when Nutty heard a terrific grunt from behind and looked back to see the man take a hard fall. Both skis were off, and he was flat on his face in the snow.

Everyone stopped. The man in red was getting up, a little slowly, and he was cursing mightily. "You see, sir," William was saying. "Anyone can fall."

But Nutty was now watching the hill. The policemen were coming fast, gaining quickly. The man in red got his skis back on, but before he could get going, a voice came from behind. "All right, Pritchard, just drop those ski poles and put your hands on the back of your head. You too, Bates."

Nutty saw a startled look come over the two men's faces, but they complied; and when he looked over at William, he had a big grin on his face.

"It's lucky that he finally fell," Nutty said. "I didn't dare try it again."

"Well, no, I didn't either," William said. "But that's why it seemed such a good idea to fall across his skis and release his bindings as I was getting up."

Chapter 13

All the Truth

The boys were sitting in the lobby of their lodge. Mr. Fullmer was with them. Pritchard and Bates were handcuffed and locked in a police car outside, and the two policemen, with help from two more, were digging in the snow where the boys said they would find the documents.

Mr. Fullmer was staring at the floor, obviously disheartened. He was quiet for some time, and then he looked up and said, "I'm really sorry that I put you boys at such a risk. It was the wrong thing to do."

"Mr. Fullmer," William said, "would you mind telling us what's going on? It seems to me that you do owe us an explanation."

Fullmer nodded, and then in a moment he said, "Well, you were helping a thief, I'm afraid. At least that's what I almost turned out to be." He stared steadily at the floor. "I'm an engineer—for a big computer company. I have access to the designs for some new hardware my company is planning to put on the market in another year or so. There are lots of people in the world who want those plans. It's advantageous to have the first software compatible with a major computer system like ours."

"So you stole those plans to sell them to someone?" Orlando said. He seemed shocked.

Fullmer didn't like to think of himself that way; Nutty could see that. He looked over at Orlando sadly. "Yes. But I didn't go through with it."

"Why not?"

"That's not easy to say. I've had some terrible luck this year. I'm in real financial trouble, and I thought I saw a way out of it. But I started to have second thoughts almost as soon as I got on the airplane to fly here to Utah."

"Why were you making the exchange at a ski resort anyway?" William asked.

"Well, I'm an avid skier. I usually take a trip or two in the winter somewhere to ski—so it was a natural enough way to handle it. It was my own idea."

"What changed your mind?" William asked. "Why didn't you just sell the papers and go home?"

"I'm not sure I know. I felt guilty and scared— involved in something really wrong. I told myself that I was only giving one company a little head start over another and that wasn't such a big deal. But I didn't really believe that. And then I met with Lott —the one you know as Mr. Spencer—and I really didn't like him."

"What difference did that make?" Nutty said.

"I guess it shouldn't have made any. If you're a thief, you're a thief. But he seemed to symbolize what I was becoming. He didn't care about anyone or anything—he just wanted the designs. So at that point I started to hedge a little. I didn't really say that I had changed my mind, but he could see that I was getting edgy. That's when he got really ugly. He made some frightening threats—not just to me but to my family. And he made one mistake. He admitted that he was representing a communist government. I had thought it was just some computer company. It was hard enough to see myself as a thief without having to think of myself as a traitor besides."

"But I don't understand," William said. "How would the designs help a communist country?"

"We're way ahead in the computer field, William. The communists get almost all of their high technology from us. The hardware in those designs will have some very handy functions for certain weapons. I suppose the communists feel they can't afford to wait a year or two to get their hands on something like that."

"I see. So when you stashed the documents, you were trying to find a way to get out of the deal?"

"That's right. I told Lott that I had left the papers in Salt Lake City, that I didn't want to be walking around with them until I was sure about our deal. So I promised to go into town and return with them. By then he had become suspicious. He said that I could go after the documents; but there was no doubt in my mind that he would follow me. That's when he first introduced me to Pritchard and Bates. I guess he wanted me to see that he had some muscle with him."

"Why did you decide to put the designs in the drain pipe?" Bilbo asked.

"Looking back on it, that was not a very good decision. But I only had a couple of minutes. I knew that if I did manage to shake Spencer and the other two, sooner or later they would want to search the room. That meant they would find the designs. So I thought my best bet was to put them where someone would discover them, and then to leave the note and ask for help."

"Why didn't you take them with you?"

"I didn't dare. Not with the likelihood that Lott would follow me. If I tried to get away from him and he did catch up with me somehow, my only bargaining power would be to know where those papers were. Once he had them, I didn't know what he might do to me. And if I destroyed them, I wouldn't have anything to try to buy my life with."

"Why didn't you finish the note?"

"I was interrupted. Pritchard and Bates came to my door and pressed me to get going. I think they were trying to make it very clear that I had better not try anything. So I left. I drove into town and parked my rental car. They didn't even try to hide the fact that they were following me. But I walked into the front door of a hotel and out the back door. Then I went to another hotel on foot and checked in under a false name."

"Wait a minute," William said. "I don't see what all this was accomplishing."

"I just wanted to get away from those people and then figure something out. I thought about going to the police, but I was still hoping to get out of the whole thing without anyone finding out what I had almost done."

"But you sure put us in a bad position."

"I know. And that's what started to worry me. I came back up the next morning and tried to reach you. I wanted to get hold of the papers and get out of there if I could. I didn't know whether I'd be safe back home—or anywhere after that—but there was one thing I had decided for sure during the night: no matter what happened, they were not getting those designs."

"I see," William said, nodding, as though all these possibilities had crossed his mind before. "You checked at the desk at that point, I suppose, and got our message. Why didn't you stay at the ticket booth?"

"I saw Pritchard and Bates, watched them long enough to see that it was you they were following. That's when I assumed that somehow they had guessed that I had left the papers. Otherwise, they would be searching for me, not following someone else."

"Yes, we said too much when we first found them, I'm afraid. They were in the next room, and I'm sure they were using some sort of listening device."

"Well, they must have decided to tail you and see if I met you for an exchange. I'm sure they checked at the desk and got the same message I did. That's probably why they didn't move in on you. They wanted the documents, but at that point, they also wanted me. They couldn't afford to have me running around, knowing what I knew. All the same, I tried all day to find some way to get to you, but they were always around. So I finally contacted the police."

"You called that day?"

"Not until evening, after I saw Lott jump off your balcony. At that point, I knew they had come out in the open and I had to do something. I'm the one who told the police who Lott really was. I also set up a plan with the police to catch Pritchard and Bates."

"A plan?" Nutty said. "What kind of plan?"

"We were going to let you ski, but policemen were going to follow you. We wanted Pritchard and Bates to make some direct contact. Our problem was, we had no real proof of anything. Lott had his story—his word against yours—and Pritchard and Bates could give their word against mine. We needed something more. The police actually went to your room to let you know what they were doing, but by then you had managed to sneak out. And they probably didn't dare approach you on the slopes, for fear of scaring off Pritchard and Bates. I'm afraid your clever little trick on the tram almost blew the whole thing."

"Yes, well—we did do a good job of that." William grinned.

Orlando was mumbling. "I don't believe this. We could have walked out the door, and you made us jump. You could have gotten us killed. Geez, William, I'm not going to listen to you anymore. You and your stupid plans."

"I wouldn't say that," Mr. Fullmer said. "William's little trick of dropping the documents in the snow was awfully smart. I wish I had thought of the same thing. I could have saved all of you a lot of trouble."

Soon after that the police came in. They had the papers. And they took Mr. Fullmer away. The boys felt bad for him—hoped things would go all right—but they also felt greatly relieved. Nutty had the feeling he could breathe again for the first time in three days.

When they got to their room, they all dropped down on the beds and chairs, and just sort of looked at each other. "I can't believe all the stuff we've been through," Bilbo said. "This was supposed to be a relaxing vacation."

Orlando nodded, looking very serious—as though he were imitating William. "Well, it could have been worse," he said. "You can thank me that those guys are on their way to jail right now."

"What?"

"Sure. All those fake falls I made were just to stall those guys—so the cops could catch up."

"Come on," Nutty said. "Those weren't fake, and you know it. I watched you take some real crashes."

"Hey, what good is a fake fall if it looks fake? I made 'em look real. I've been telling you all along that looking like a skier is not the same as being a skier. Well, it's the same thing the other way. You've gotta know how not to look like one."

William was chuckling. "Excellent," he said. "Orlando, if you're in that kind of control now, you should do very well the rest of the trip. I doubt you'll ever fall again—except when you choose to, of course."

But Orlando still looked entirely serious. "Hey, right. Except—I'll probably switch from looking good to being good sometimes, and then back. I'm not one of those show-off types who ski around like a ballet dancer all the time."

Nutty was rolling his eyes, and Bilbo was about to tell Orlando what he thought of the way he "looked" when someone knocked on the door. Everyone looked a little hesitant, as though something terrible were about to start happening all over again. But then the voice of Mrs. Ash boomed through the door. "Are you fellows in there?"

Nutty got up and opened the door. "Hello, Mrs. Ash," he said, very politely.

"Well, I'm glad to find you guys. Are you coming to lunch with us?"

"Oh, sure," Nutty said.

"Frankly, I'm disappointed with all of you—especially you, Nutty. You're supposed to be in charge of this trip, and most of the time I can't even locate you. And now Mr. Crawford tells me you've gotten yourselves in some sort of trouble."

"Well, ma'am, we've had a couple of things come up that were a little out of the ordinary."

"Yes, well, I think it's been laziness more than anything. While everyone else has been out learning to ski, you boys have hardly done anything."

Nutty smiled, and he glanced around at the other boys. "Well, I don't know. We haven't exactly had a dull time."

Bilbo began to laugh. William nodded in that grandpa's way of his. "If you have just a minute, Mrs. Ash, I have quite a story to tell you."

But Orlando stood up. "No, no. Allow me. Let me tell you how I caught the dangerous ski-slope spies."

HEARST FREE LIBRARY
ANACONDA, MONTANA